BEYOND DREAM

BEYOND DREAM

A.S. GODIN

Library of Congress Control Number: 2024918531
Paperback ISBN: 979-8-9913967-2-1
Hardcover Book ISBN: 979-8-9913967-9-0
eBook ISBN: 979-8-9913967-1-4
Audiobook ISBN: 979-8-9913967-8-3

Published by Godin Books
Printed in the USA

To Adelina, Emma, and James

Adelina, my niece, and the two friends she made camping one spring at Succor Creek were the children who helped come up with some of the dreams I used for inspiration. I told them if it ever got published, their names would be inside.

—A.S.

"If you never dream, you will never know the endless possibilities of what you can become."

— ANNETTE WHITE

CHAPTER

ONE

"Colossal, look," Maera said to the gigantic reptile dozing beside her as she pointed toward the dark Forest of Screams and Shadows. The great dragon stirred next to her, waking from his nap. His glossy black scales glinted like thousands of fire-licked jewels across his massive body. Lazily, the great dragon turned and blinked intelligent, golden eyes at her before letting out a big, smoky yawn, exposing long, glistening, sharp teeth. His gleaming scales flashed with each movement, reflecting the colorful skies streaked with daunting oranges and reds, like sunsets before a big storm. The sky cast the land in ominous colors, frightening most who looked upon it like the great dragon himself. The entire horizon was blanketed in colors of red, and closer to the forest, the clouds gathered and darkened into heavy, pregnant grays, threatening to unleash their fury upon the misty, gloomy forest beneath.

Daytime was a mix of red, angry skies, or the colors of a fierce storm, whereas the night was a starry sky obscured by pockets of clouds, permitting only a small amount of the hazy moon to ever peek out, giving the landscape a haunted feeling. The dismal sky wasn't what caught her eye, though. No, it was the boy who raced toward the forest itself.

"There, Colossal," Maera gestured again toward the dark forest. They could just make out the boy's form, made clearer by his bright, pale hair as he ran from the ugly witch who chased him.

The black dragon finally glanced down, stretching his long, spiked neck to peer at the valley below. The friends were perched on a brown, rocky ledge that jutted out from the Mountains of Terror. Many steep ledges and sharp rocks made an imposing, twisted mountain border around the land of Nightmare. It was one of the best views of the land, and from there, Maera could see everything.

Maera watched the boy with white-blond hair and red-and-blue pajamas run from Old Hagetha. She was one of the scariest witches in Nightmare, the land of bad dreams. Maera lived in Nightmare, and it was all she had known for as long as she could remember.

"Do you think Ol' Hagetha will catch him?" Maera asked Colossal. Colossal narrowed his eyes until he almost squinted. He snorted, causing smoke to puff out of his nose, before giving a quick nod. Though Colossal couldn't speak words, Maera had no trouble understanding him.

"Maybe you're right," Maera sighed. "Then again, he's got a good head start." *The boy is fast... faster than the other children that often come to Nightmare.* "Do you think he'll wake up? Or stay a while in Nightmare?"

Colossal growled and then hissed before snapping his large jaw and letting a low, rumbling noise crawl up his golden chest.

"He might wake up," Maera argued. "Some can do that, you know." After another tense moment of watching, she tapped her chin in thought. "I think we should get closer. I've seen him before. I want to know what he'll do if she catches him," Maera declared.

Colossal growled a warning, voicing his disapproval at the idea.

"I know, I know. I'm not planning to interfere," Maera swore with a hand over her heart. She wasn't supposed to interfere with a Hunt. A Hunt was a nightmare where a Sleeper would get chased down and tormented. They called the people who visited the Land of Dreams *Sleepers*. They either found themselves in Nightmare or Dream but disappeared from the realm the moment they woke up. Maera never visited Dream. Those who lived in Dream stayed in that realm, while those who lived in Nightmare stayed in Nightmare, where she lived.

"He looks pretty scared," Maera noted as she watched the boy run from the witch.

Since this was Hagetha's hunt, Maera couldn't get involved. Even though there were a select few Sleepers who knew how to wake themselves up if they got too scared, no one else was allowed to interrupt the dream. All Sleepers' nightmares must play out without interference from other Wonders because a Sleeper would get more out of a nightmare if it ran its course. Her father, King of Nightmares, said that was important. It had something to do with Sleepers facing their fears and working through things to better understand their real lives and the world they lived in, the Waking World.

If only I could go there, but Wonders couldn't leave the Land of Dreams. Only Sleepers could leave when they woke up.

"Oh! Look," Maera pointed. Finally, the boy reached the first line of trees, racing directly into the dark forest. "If he stays in there, he's sure to get so scared that Hagetha might catch him, and I want to see if she does. Brigga failed the last time the boy came here, so I want to see if Hagetha can do it."

Colossal snorted again. Maera pushed away from the rocky

cliff face of the Mountains of Terror, standing and dusting off her hands.

"Come on, Colossal. I want to get a closer look–I promise I won't interfere. I just want to see if Hagetha will catch him. If she does, do you think she will scratch at him, scream at him, or maybe try and eat him?" Before Colossal could respond, Maera frowned. "Hmmm. Maybe she won't try to eat him. That's more Sinda's style." Sinda was another witch who lived in the Forest of Screams and Shadows.

Colossal yawned, and a heated, fiery breath escaped and shimmered as heat waves in the air before he snapped his sharp, white teeth together with one final snort.

"You're right. Ol' Hagetha likes to claw at the Sleepers with her ugly, sharp nails. I still want to see, though." This boy had dreamed of witches before. Sometimes, it had been in the House of Familiarity, a house near the edge of the forest that transformed to look like the Sleeper's house in the Waking World. This boy visited Nightmare more often lately. Maera was curious to know why. Many Sleepers only visit Nightmare occasionally, spending most of their nights in Dream.

Maera had first seen the boy through the upper bedroom window of the House of Familiarity. He had woken in Nightmare in a bedroom that looked just like his, and Brigga tried to scare him by hovering above his bed in her dress of shadows. She was good at that. Her fingers were gnarled, crooked, and long. Despite her efforts, the boy slipped out of bed and ran outside. Then he did something Maera hadn't seen in a long time. He leaped into the air and flew... *without* wings. When he reached the stars, he woke and disappeared.

The second time the boy dreamed of witches, Sinda tried to lure him into her cottage. Her cottage always seemed warm and inviting compared to the scary forest. It was nestled deep inside the forest and at the first glimpse, looked safe, providing a haven from all the creepy creatures, the moans and screams, and the shadows that played tricks on the mind. But her cottage was a trap, and once she lured a Sleeper inside, Sinda would try to put the Sleeper into a big pie and cook it in the large oven to eat as a snack. When Sinda tried this with the boy, he woke up just before she draped the crust over him.

"Let's go," Maera said as she patted Colossal on his massive shoulder. He lowered his large, leathery wing so she could climb up on top of him. He stood as tall as two horses and was as long as a bus. She had to arrange her red and black dress to sit on top of him. Thankfully, she had thought to wear her black leggings underneath. Once she was comfortable, she held onto the Colossal's long neck spikes as he rose onto his thick hind legs, using his wings like elbows to crawl to the cliff's edge. He jumped off, and his beautiful black wings unfolded, catching the wind until they soared through the air toward the forest. Maera's long, curly brown hair worked itself out of her braid and fluttered in the wind behind her.

"Hurry," Maera urged. Colossal tucked his wings closer to his body, and they dove. The ground got closer, as did the trees. He expanded his wings once more, and then they skimmed along the tops of the trees.

"There!" Maera called out, pointing to the boy who was weaving in between the trees. Hagetha was close on his tail, cackling with twisted glee as she chased after her prey. In Nightmare, Hagetha was the hunter, and the boy was the hunted. Screams and moans echoed from inside the eerie forest, affirming its proper name, the Forest of Screams and Shadows. The shadows played tricks on the eyes. Sometimes, glowing eyes would shine from inside of them. Sometimes, the shadows took the shape of monsters. The wind passed through the leaves and branches, sounding like screams and moans, making the shadows more terrifying.

"Get me closer," Maera ordered. "You can land in the meadow. He's heading right for it." Colossal flew toward the Meadow of Mist, a clearing inside the dark, dense forest. Once he landed, a few ghosts closed in on Maera. The tall grass was slick with condensation from the mist that swirled around them, and the tops brushed against the back of Colossal's knees. Strange noises echoed in the foggy meadow, making it seem more frightening to Sleepers. Ghosts moaned and groaned, sometimes using the mist to sneak right up and torment you. Sometimes, they reached through the fog to touch a shoulder, pull hair, or grab an arm for scares. Maera waved them all off.

"Not now," Maera ordered impatiently. "Wait until the boy gets here." She slid down the scaly side of Colossal, landing on her feet. "Otherwise, he won't be surprised." The ghosts melted back into the mist. Maera pushed her hair out of her face and stepped toward the trees, but Colossal's rumbled warning stopped her.

"I *know*," Maera rolled her eyes. "I'm not interfering. I just want a better spot to watch." Colossal grunted his dismay at the idea but backed away, blending into the shadows.

Maera ran toward the forest when she heard Hagetha and the boy. She quickly climbed one of the dark, twisted trees. As she ascended, the octopus-like branches tugged at her red skirt, which she quickly yanked free. She found a sturdy branch and settled herself, calming her breathing and holding very still.

Hagetha cackled, and her gnarled fingers with long, chipped nails reached for the boy, but he was fast—too fast. The relentless witch didn't give up, and she floated after him, something only a few creatures in Nightmare could do. Witches, ghosts, and shadow monsters all hovered without wings.

"Come here, child, let's play," Hagetha called out. Her voice was sharp and unnaturally high-pitched. Her voice grated on Sleepers' ears, causing the hair on the back of their necks to stand up, chilling them to the bone.

The boy was almost to the meadow.

You can do it! Maera thought, not daring to speak. She leaned forward, trying to see through the shadows of the trees. As the boy ran, the shadows shifted and changed. Some showed glowing eyes, while others mimicked shadow monsters, forming scary shapes, even though they were only shadows. The boy swerved away from the one with the glowing eyes, and Maera had to cover her mouth as she snickered. Now, they headed right toward her tree.

Perfect!

Just as he raced by, Maera leaned too far forward, and the branch she had held onto snapped. With a squeak of surprise, Maera tumbled to the ground, her skirt snagging and ripping as she fell. She landed on her back with a thump.

Startled, the fair-haired boy screamed. He stopped when he got a good look at her.

She blinked in surprise as she waited to catch her breath.

"Wait, y—you... you're like *me*," the boy stuttered. "Help me," he pleaded.

Maera was in for it now. She wasn't supposed to interfere, but up close, she saw how frightened he was.

Hagetha drew nearer; her shrieks and cackling laughter drifted eerily through the trees.

Maera scrambled to her feet but wasn't sure what to do. *I should run and leave him here, but... he looks so frightened.*

"Please," the boy begged with desperation pooling in his blue eyes.

"Fine. Come with me." Maera reached and took the boy's hand. She dragged him toward the darkest shadows.

"Wait, no, not there," the boy implored, struggling against her hold.

"Trust me," Maera said, and then she ran, keeping a firm grip on the boy's hand.

The boy followed despite his urge to run from the shadows full of glowing eyes. The boy tightly squeezed her hand tighter as they fled through the gloomy silhouettes. They raced past the rocks, bushes, trees, and shadows. They ran until they reached an old, gnarled tree far bigger than any others in the forest. It had no leaves and looked like it could come alive at any moment, grabbing whoever dared to get too close.

"I don't think this is a good idea," the boy said, but Maera silently towed him after her. She rounded the side of the tree until she found the large split in the trunk that was wider toward the base.

"In here," Maera whispered, dropping the boy's hand and crawling through the large crack in the tree.

The boy hesitated but followed when he heard the witch's voice closing in.

"Oh, *child*! Come play with me," Hagetha called with a shrill voice that cut like glass. She got closer. "Come be my little pet." Her terrible cackle caused the boy to drop to his hands and knees and quickly crawl through the crack in the tree's base. Inside, Maera held her finger to her lips, urging the boy to be quiet.

"Child... where *are* you? Come out so I can chase you down, you little runt!" Hagetha's voice drifted around the tree while she searched. Immediately, the boy placed his hand over the top of Maera's as he trembled with fear.

"Come out, come out, wherever you are," Hagetha beckoned. "Let's play a game!"

The boy searched Maera's eyes, but Maera merely shook her head.

"A game where I squeeze the breath out of you! Boy? Where are you?" Hagetha continued looking. When she wandered closer to the tree, the concealed children pressed themselves against the inside trunk of the tree, remaining hidden within.

Eventually, Hagetha moved on but continued searching for her prey.

The boy and Maera waited until the witch's voice grew quieter the further away she hunted. When they couldn't hear her anymore, Maera smiled.

"Thanks," the boy sighed with relief. "Thanks for saving me. I'm Theodore, but my friends call me Theo."

"I'm Maera. Just Maera."

"You look like me. Does that mean you're having a nightmare, too?" Theo asked.

"No. I live here."

"You *live* here?" Theo retorted with his eyebrows nearly leaving his forehead.

"Yes."

"But... isn't it *scary*?" Theo whispered.

Maera smiled. "Not to me."

"Does that make you one of *them*?" He pointed in Hagetha's direction.

Maera shrugged her shoulders. "I guess so."

"So...." Theo scooted away from her, inching closer to the opening of the tree. "Does that mean you're going to try scaring me, or will you try and hurt me? I mean, this is a nightmare, isn't it?"

Maera frowned. "Yes. I mean, no."

"Well, which is it?" Theo demanded; his eyes widened as he waited for her answer.

"This is the Land of Nightmare, but I won't hurt you," Maera confessed. "I should probably go now, though. I shouldn't have saved you; I'm not supposed to do that." Maera pushed past Theo and crawled out from inside the tree's trunk. She brushed the dirt from her red and black dress.

"Wait! Where are you going?" Theo called after her.

"I'm not supposed to interfere with people's nightmares," Maera said over her shoulder.

"Why?" he asked, trotting after her; a trail of dust billowed behind him as clumps of dirt fell from his pajamas.

"Because my father said that it's bad, but I didn't mean to."

"Didn't mean to what?" Theo questioned.

"You know, interrupt your nightmare?" Maera clarified, slowing enough that Theo could catch up. "I was watching from the tree, and the branch broke, which is why I fell." Maera stopped to face Theo.

"Then where will you go? Are you just going to leave me here? Alone? In this creepy forest? What if that scary witch comes back?"

"Whoa!" Maera balked. "You have a lot of questions."

"I do. Like, what now? And why can't you stay for a little while longer?" Theo fired back.

"Weren't you saying a second ago that I might scare you or hurt you?" Maera put her hands on her hips.

"Well, yeah," Theo scratched his arm. "You said you're from here, so I just thought...," his voice trailed off.

Maera turned and marched toward the Meadow of Mist, where Colossal waited.

"Hey," Theo said, running to catch up. "I'm sorry."

"For what?" Maera asked.

"For thinking you might hurt me. I just thought, since this *is* a nightmare, you might turn into a monster and scare me, too. I'm sorry if I got that wrong."

"It doesn't matter," Maera flatly stated. "I shouldn't have intervened. I shouldn't have gotten in Hagetha's way. I wasn't supposed to do that."

"I'm glad you did," Theo said. "That was nice of you. Thanks."

Maera stopped and looked back at Theo.

Theo paused and sheepishly kicked at the dirt. "I really thought she'd get me," he added.

Maera turned around and kept trekking toward the meadow with Theo in hot pursuit.

"You can't follow me," Maera informed him.

"Why?"

Maera frowned and then spun and faced him. "I'll get in trouble. If you follow me, everyone will know I helped you when I shouldn't have."

Theo looked surprised. "So, you'll get punished? Really?"

"Yes." She began walking again. "So, stop following me." Maera tried to sound bossy, but Theo easily caught up, following her toward the Meadow of Mist.

When they pushed through the fog, the ghosts instantly appeared, separating from the mist that hovered above the long cheatgrass. Their moaning and groaning loomed closer, happy to have a Sleeper to torment.

"W—wha—what is that?" Theo stammered.

Maera trudged on, swishing her arms and waving off the ghosts while searching for her dragon.

"Maera? Are those ghosts?" Theo asked while pointing to a couple of phantoms that floated closer to him. As they reached for him with their glass-like hands, Theo squeaked, "Maera?" He froze. "Maera!" His feet were stuck in place like he was sinking in quicksand; he couldn't move. "Maera, please...."

Maera stopped and turned, huffing with frustration. "I'm not supposed to help."

"Please," Theo begged. "Don't leave me here with them."

Theo looked so helpless and so alone. Maera grumbled a complaint under her breath, knowing she was about to make another big mistake. Turning on her heel, she stomped back to Theo and grabbed his hand. "Enough!" she barked, and all the ghosts scattered, disappearing into the mist. She pulled Theo behind her.

"I think they're gone now," Theo said breathlessly. "How come they listen to you?"

"The ghosts?" Maera asked.

Theo nodded.

"Well," she thought about it for a moment. "I guess it's because I'm from here. None of them can *really* hurt me. They might try if they thought they could, but I've been here long enough that they don't scare me anymore."

"I wish *I* weren't afraid," Theo confessed.

"And what would you do if you weren't?" Maera wanted to know.

Theo shrugged. "I guess I would try and help others who were scared. First, I would fight back and make sure the nightmares couldn't hurt me or anyone else. Then, if I could, I would make it so that no one ever had another nightmare again."

"If you did that, this place," Maera spread her arm out, gesturing to the world around her, "Nightmare wouldn't exist... and neither would I."

"Oh," Theo frowned. "I didn't think of that." Then, a smile tugged at his lips. "I know! You said this is Nightmare, where nightmares happen. So, doesn't that mean there's a land of good dreams? Where are all the good dreams?"

"In Dream," Maera answered. "That realm is past the Ocean of Despair and the Mountains of Terror. I'm not allowed to go there."

"Why?"

"Because I'm a Wonder in Nightmare, which means I belong here. I don't belong in Dream."

Theo's brows drew together. "What's a Wonder?"

"A Wonder is any creature born in The Land of Dreams. Since I was born here, I'm a Nightmare Wonder. Those born in

Dream are Dream Wonders. Nightmares don't mix with dreams."

"They don't?" Theo frowned.

Maera thought for a moment and then shook her head. "I don't think so. I was always told to never cross into Dream, or I might disappear."

"What if I took you there? Could you go if I went with you? Maybe it's different if you go there with me since I'm not from here."

"I... I'm not sure," Maera said hesitantly.

"We could try! If you were there in Dream, you could help me stop others from having nightmares. Then I could come back and help people escape their nightmares! Since you'd be in Dream, you wouldn't disappear if this place no longer existed! You'd be safe!"

Maera's lips pressed together. "I'm not sure that it works like that." *And what about all my friends?* She didn't want them to disappear.

"Why not?" Theo questioned.

Before she could answer, a roar shook the ground as Colossal came out of the shadows. Colossal had heard every word they'd said and wasn't happy. Maera feared he would tell on her to her father.

"You have to go, Theo," Maera hissed. "You've upset Colossal by talking about ending nightmares."

"What do you mean? What is that? What's a Colossal?"

"He's a dragon... a dragon who knows you want to put an end to Nightmare," Maera answered. "You need to go. Can you wake yourself up?"

"N—no—not usually," Theo stuttered.

"Then run, NOW!"

"But what about you?" Theo asked while he backed away.

"I'll be fine, I think," Maera replied. She likely would get in huge trouble now with her father. Colossal was sure to tell him everything.

Another roar ripped through the air, shaking the ground again. This time, Colossal stomped toward them. The fog hid him enough to make him look like a large shadow that got darker as he drew nearer.

"Hurry, Theo. You need to run."

Colossal emerged, and his massive black form cut through the mist, which curled and swirled around him like wisps of white smoke. He sucked in a breath, and his golden chest glowed; he was about to breathe fire.

"Run!" Maera shouted.

Seconds later, the dragon's mouth was open, and the building inferno was ready to be released.

Theo took one look at Colossal and then ran.

Colossal blasted a jet of fire, but Theo dodged it, avoiding being burned.

"Colossal, don't," Maera warned, but Colossal only answered to the king. Now, Colossal felt it was his duty to properly scare Theo. Maera had interrupted Theo's nightmare, so it was up to Colossal to fix it. The great dragon drew in another big breath, and the blistering blaze glowed within his chest. Just as Colossal was about to unleash his fire, Maera jumped in front of Theo.

Theo turned to see where the massive dragon was, and he saw Maera's daring move. "Maera! Look out!" Theo cried just as the burning flames blasted toward them.

Maera lifted her hand. The moment the fire reached her, she thrust her hand outward, causing the fire to split and move around herself and Theo.

"You need to run!" Maera told Theo. "I can't hold him off for long!"

Theo didn't answer, so she turned to face him.

He had disappeared.

Maera put down her hand and sighed in relief.

TWO

Colossal roared and growled in anger. Maera hung her head in shame while he lectured her. She had interfered—something she was forbidden to do—something she'd said she wouldn't do. Colossal grumbled, hissed, and snapped his teeth until he had nothing more to say.

"I know," Maera said miserably. "But I couldn't help it. It was an accident."

Colossal snarled and rumbled in the language of dragons. He emphasized that she'd fallen, helped Theo hide, and stuck with him after Hagetha had left. She had helped the boy in the meadow, which was no *accident*. He glared at her with angry, bright golden eyes, driving home his point with one final snort of smoke.

"I know!" Maera declared. "It's just that Theo looked so lost and so scared. I couldn't help it. I swear, it was only this one time, and I won't interrupt a Sleeper's nightmare again."

Colossal snorted and adjusted his wings in what would look like a human crossing their arms. He didn't believe a word she said.

"I mean it," Maera argued.

Colossal stomped up to her, dropping his leathery wing and snapping his sharp teeth impatiently.

"All right, all right. I'll get on." Maera didn't look forward to what was coming. Colossal was taking her home, where he would have to tell her father what she'd done. She dragged her feet.

The dragon jerked his head, signaling her to hurry.

"All right," Maera sighed, then finally climbed up.

Once Maera was seated on his shoulders and had a proper handhold of his neck's black spikes, Colossal ran, pumping his wings, and he took off. They climbed high into the sky and angled to the Black Castle. The fortress stood on top of a huge lava hill. The hill was called a butte and had formed long ago from the now-sleeping volcano nearby. The castle's black exterior starkly contrasted the reds and oranges of the distant volcanoes behind it that glowed with fire and spouts of lava.

Smoke curled around the base of the castle from the Fire Forest that constantly burned. The Fire and Ash Wonders lived in the Fire Forest. There were ash worms, firebirds, and burned monsters with glowing orange eyes. Maera thought it was beautiful, though many thought the burning forest was terrifying.

The castle on the hill grew bigger as they flew closer. Tall black spires reached from multiple levels, and the many windows glittered like dark blue jewels. The towers jutted from the mountain hundreds of feet into the air, pointing into the starlit sky with its dark red peaked roofs. The black stone glistened in the firelight of the forest and distant volcanoes, reflecting reds and oranges.

When they flew above the castle, Colossal tucked in his black wings and dove toward the gate. Maera hung on while the warm wind whipped at her face and brown hair. Colossal spread his wings, bowing them like a parachute to slow their descent until he floated the rest of the way to the ground. He landed gently before the stone castle's large, metal-studded doors. Their dark purple color looked almost black. Maera released a long sigh and looked into the sky, not wanting to face her father. Growing impatient, Colossal shook his body, and Maera slid off his cool scales.

"Okay! I'm going!" she huffed.

He responded with a snort and a growl.

Maera trudged up to the castle entrance, where two shadow monsters opened the thick doors for her. The huge metal studs glimmered as she passed through; Colossal followed on her heels while she lumbered through the large rooms, passing the werewolf guards in their tarnished armor. Some rooms were furnished with dark teal with black accents and had plush couches, ornate rugs, and large hearths with strikingly carved wooden mantels. The fires burned orange or blue, depending on the room. Other rooms were decorated with midnight blue trimmed with black wooden pillars and archways displaying various art on the walls. Some rooms had beautifully dark carved wooden furnishing set inside maroon and dark purple décor. The rooms were well suited for the overall black, gothic look of the castle that Maera found stunning.

Maera wound her way through the various halls and corridors until she and Colossal reached the throne room. It was the largest room in the castle, with high arching ceilings down the center and a throne on a platform at the far end. Pillars lined either side of the room where they supported lower ceilings under which various nobles in their dark attire stood and visited with one another. The ladies wore dresses of dark blues, maroons, reds, purples, and teals trimmed with black lace. The men wore suits of similar colors. When she walked in, tailed by her large dragon, everyone stopped talking and faced the king's daughter.

Maera walked down the red carpet toward the platform where her father sat on his throne. Above the throne, a beautiful balcony held a massive hourglass that glowed from the obscured light that streamed from the circular stained-glass window behind it. Inside the hourglass, a red mist swirled around the top and dropped red sand granules that fell like snow, tumbling and funneling to the bottom. Her father had once said it was what nightmares were made of. She felt there was hardly enough to fill it these days.

Maera dropped her eyes from the hourglass to her father, who was holding a large, black wooden staff. At the top of the staff, a glowing red orb was held in place by tiny, curled talons made of wood.

"Daughter," her father's booming voice hailed as she approached. He rose from his throne, standing taller than any other creature in Nightmare. His cloak of shadows was covered in colorful nebulas and stars. His sharp, pale features stood out against the darkness of his cloak. His clean-cut beard was short, his long, glossy, black hair was tightly tied with a single cord, and his black crown rested on his head.

Maera stood at the base of the platform. Her father loomed over her while Colossal stationed himself behind her; together, they bowed to the king.

"Rise," her father barked. "Tell me what's happened."

Maera swallowed hard.

Colossal hissed, grunted, grumbled, and gnashed his teeth.

Her father listened intently as Colossal told him what Maera had done. Her father's dark eyebrows drew together in an intense scowl with every noise Colossal spewed.

"I see," the king said after a moment. "Thank you, Colossal. You may leave now."

Colossal bowed his large, scaly head.

"Everyone," the king announced. "Out!"

Murmurs erupted as people left. Colossal crawled out of the throne room after them, walking on his two hind legs and folded wings he used like arms.

Maera was alone with the King of Nightmares.

"Maera," the king beckoned. "Come here."

Maera walked up the three steps to the throne. Her father turned away from her and climbed the ornate spiral stairs leading to the balcony above. Maera silently followed. When they got to the top, her father walked around the massive hourglass. She glanced at the red cloud, watching the grains of sand, each catching the light as they fell.

"Look," her father urged, pointing his staff at the trickle of red sand. "Do you see this?"

"Yes," Maera nodded.

"What does it look like to you?" he inquired.

"It looks like red sand, though there's not a whole lot in there right now," Maera noticed.

Her father frowned for a moment before he turned back to the large glass structure. "It *is* sand," he agreed. "What you see falling is the sand created whenever someone has a nightmare. This comes from their imagination. It's because of nightmares that we exist. This sand is collected as long as Sleepers create new nightmares. We become what the Sleepers seek, what they need. Do you know how important it is that Sleepers have nightmares?"

Maera shook her head. "No."

"If that boy found a way to prevent nightmares from happening, we would disappear, all of us. Without nightmares, dreams would also disappear. Do you know how important it is for Sleepers to dream?"

"Isn't it to help them work out problems in the Waking World?" Maera asked.

"Yes. Dreams and nightmares exist to help the Sleepers face difficulties in a protected world where their bodies won't get hurt."

Maera tilted her head. "But don't nightmares hurt Sleepers?"

"The Sleepers think so, but in truth, only fear makes it feel real. It is their *imagination* that makes it possible. Imagination can be a powerful tool or weapon, and it's the foundation our world is built upon."

"But then, why would anyone want a nightmare?" Maera reasoned.

"No one *wants* a nightmare, daughter, but they're no less important than a dream. Nightmares help Sleepers face their fears. They help Sleepers learn to overcome hardships or difficult things. They help Sleepers become stronger and braver so they can better face the Waking World and the problems that arise there."

Maera's head drooped. "So... I made it so that Theo couldn't be brave? Or strong?"

"In a way, yes. So far, young Theo has only run from his nightmares. He will never learn by running from his fears. He must learn to face them," her father answered.

"But he was so scared. He asked me to help," Maera argued. "I didn't feel right about leaving him."

"I know. That's because you're a good girl. Sometimes, doing the right thing is hard. After all, nightmares also help Sleepers dream of happier things. That's important, too. One can't exist without the other. So, by taking away his nightmare, you've also taken away a dream."

Maera felt guilt pull down on her shoulders. She didn't want to take away a dream. She'd heard of dreams. They were supposed to be happy, fun, and magical. She'd never been to Dream, where all the good dreams are from, but she'd heard stories.

"I did a bad thing then," Maera said quietly. "I just thought maybe he wouldn't be scared if I helped. I didn't know it made it so he didn't get a dream."

"My sweet Night Maera." Her father placed a gentle hand on her shoulder, using the special nickname only he called her. "It's all about balance. That is why it is so important that Wonders never interfere with a Sleeper's nightmare or dream unless they are a part of that dream. Nightmares and dreams must play out until the Sleeper is ready to wake. Otherwise, the Sleeper won't learn the lesson that a dream or nightmare brings. Luckily, some sand was still collected from his nightmare, so it isn't a total loss."

"I really didn't mean to interrupt the nightmare," Maera confessed with a trembling lip. "I fell. It was an accident." She hated getting in trouble. She hated it even more when she disappointed her father. Her eyes stung with unshed tears.

The king smiled a sad smile. He gently brushed his thumb over her cheek, catching a runaway tear. "I know, little one. I know you don't mean to. You are my little Wonder. My little Night Maera. I know that often you don't like following the rules, but I hope that now you'll understand why Sleepers need nightmares. Now that you know, you can make better choices from this point on."

"I'll do better," she promised. "I will."

Her father nodded. "I know you will. Now, would you like to stay while I use some sand to make new Wonders? Since there's more sand in the glass, I think I'll have enough to make a brand-new nightmare."

"You mean I actually get to watch you make a nightmare!?" Maera clapped with excitement. She'd always known the sand inside the hourglass was important, but her father had never shown her how or why.

"Yes. If you would like."

"I would!" Maera exclaimed with delight.

"Very well." Her father circled the hourglass to the large stained-glass window. He tapped it with his staff, and suddenly, the circular window disappeared, opening the space to the world beyond. From this spot, all of Nightmare was laid before the king. The sky was a dusky blue and sprinkled with many stars. Close to the snowy mountains in the distance, the sky lightened, and the clouds were tinged with pink and purple. In Nightmare, the clouds looked gray and black, sometimes hiding the many stars in the sky, only allowing them to peek through patches here and there.

"I can see the Valley of Horrors from up here! Oh, and the Mountains of Terror and the Forest of Screams and Shadows! Look! There's the Ghost Town and the Carnival of Creeps! And there's the Haunted Plains, where all the graveyards are, and over there, I can see the Roads of Wreckage." The Roads of Wreckage was the only part of Nightmare she wasn't allowed to go to.

The King of Nightmares laughed. "Yes, from here, you can see all of Nightmare. Now, with my staff, I can take the Sand of Imagination from inside the hourglass and create new nightmares. Like this...." Her father tapped the glass with the red orb at the end of his staff.

Maera watched as tiny, red grains of sand floated upward and turned into a flash of red light. The tendrils of light then got sucked up into the red orb, making it glow.

"Now, watch," her father said before he turned to face Nightmare. "Think of something you believe would scare someone," her father instructed.

Maera thought about something perfectly horrible... something putrid. *Zombies.* "Okay, got it," she smiled.

Her father tapped the staff on the ground twice and then held it out. Suddenly, the red light burst from the end, and a zombie appeared.

"Wow! You actually made a zombie Wonder!" *He is exactly like I imagined!* Maera thought.

The zombie looked dazed and confused.

Maera approached the newborn zombie and reached out her hand. "Hi! My name's Maera. What's yours?"

The zombie looked at her with dead yellow eyes before letting out a garbled groan.

"You don't have a name?" Maera frowned.

The zombie scratched its head, causing a few patches of hair to fall out.

"Oops! You lost some of your hair. Here." Maera bent over and picked it up. She reached up and stuck it back to the zombie's sticky head. "There. That's better. Wow, you smell *terrible*! Oh! I know! I'll call you Stinky because you smell a little... like death." Then she quickly added, "But that's a good thing here in Nightmare!"

The zombie grunted, scratching his head again and flashing a smile that was missing a few teeth. "S—St—Stink."

"Almost," Maera smiled. "Say it with me. S-T-I-N-K-Y."

"Stiiiinkkkyyy."

"Good job, Stinky!" Maera clapped. "I bet you're going to scare many Sleepers."

Stinky grinned at her again, displaying his few gray and black rotting teeth.

"Scare," he repeated.

"Father," Maera stepped up to the king. "Can we give Stinky some friends?"

Her father smiled. "Just a few. Then we have to make a nightmare for them to live in." Her father used his staff to make four more zombies, which Maera named Fleshy, Toothless, Grunt, and Groan.

"Where will they go to live?" Maera asked.

"There," her father pointed to the black mist past Ghost Town. "That needs a new nightmare. What do you think?"

"I think... maybe somewhere swampy would be neat." There was nothing there until her father took most of the remaining sand and turned it into light that his staff swallowed. Then, pointing in the direction of the nothingness, he blasted out a beam of red light. Suddenly, a scraggly forest of drooping trees appeared. The thick boughs hung low as if the trees melted. Gray moss hung from the branches, looking like the beards of old men.

The swampy ground was blanketed in pockets of mist that swirled and hovered mere feet above the ground.

"It's perfect!" Maera declared, clapping her hands. "Stinky, you and your friends are going to love it there! I just know it."

With another bright flare of her father's staff, the group of zombies was suddenly lifted into the air. The red light formed a bubble around the new Wonders, and then, in a flash, they were gone.

"Where did they go?" she asked.

"I sent them to the Swamp of Refuse to live where they can fulfill their purpose. I have a little sand left, so I will create a few more Wonders to live there."

Maera watched her father create two giant snakes and three crocodiles that he sent to the swamp, but not before Maera got to name them. The snakes, she called Stretch and Curly. The crocodiles were named Hunger, Snapper, and Chip because Chip had a chipped tooth.

"Those are all good names," the king smiled. "I think they're happy with them. Now, they will go off and scare Sleepers."

After her father sent them to live in the swamp, Maera frowned. "Father, earlier, Theo said I looked like him. How come I wasn't made to look scary like the other Wonders?"

"It's because you're special, Maera."

"Is that why I never hunt Sleepers? Is that why no one has nightmares about me?" Maera asked. They looked out the open window at the realm of Nightmare, watching Wonders busily hunt and scare Sleepers.

"Yes. You are my daughter, so you don't need to scare, hunt, or haunt Sleepers," her father answered.

"But Stinky and the others get to scare Sleepers as soon as they're born?"

"Yes," her father answered, "because I made it so."

"And I was born from the red sand, too?"

"All the Wonders in Nightmare are born from the red sand," her father said.

"And all Wonders have a purpose when they're born?"

"Yes. All Wonders that are born discover their purpose, a part that they will play in a Sleeper's nightmare. Usually, it is clear from the moment they're born."

"Then what's my purpose?" Maera asked, glancing up at her father.

His sharp jaw clenched, reminding Maera of the cliffs that jut from the Mountains of Terror. His chasmic eyes regarded her with patient wisdom.

"That, my daughter, is something you must figure out for yourself."

"Oh," she said. She gazed at the Swamp of Refuse and thought of Stinky and his new friends scaring Sleepers.

"Come, let's go. It's practically dinner time." Her father led her away from the window, tapping his staff and causing the stained glass to reappear. Since this was the first time Maera had ever been allowed on the balcony, she took one last savory look around. She mentally etched the memory of the colorful glass that formed a picture where a queen and king stood. The queen wore a beautiful white gown and a golden crown. In one hand, she held a wooden staff that looked just like her father's, except it was white with a gold orb. In her other hand, she held an hour-glass with gold sand. The other half of the window was a picture of her father, the king, in his cloak of stars and shadows. He held his staff in one hand and the hourglass with red sand in the other.

"Father," Maera called out as she raced to catch up to the king, who wound his way down the spiraled staircase. "Who is the woman in the stained-glass picture?"

"That is the Queen of Dreams. She rules over Dream like I rule over Nightmare."

"Oh. Can I meet her?" Maera asked.

The king shook his head. "She doesn't come to Nightmare. Wonders of Dream don't cross into Nightmare just as Wonders of Nightmare never cross into Dream."

"Never?"

"Not anymore," her father answered with finality. They left the throne room and wandered through the castle until they reached the dining hall, where a long banquet table awaited their arrival.

"Why?" Maera replied. "Why can't we cross into the other realm? Why can't the Wonders of Dream cross into ours?"

"That is simply the way it is. Sleepers don't dream like they used to. The Waking World is changing, which means the Land of Dreams is changing too. One day, you'll understand." They sat at the table and waited for their meal without discussing it further.

THREE

A whole week passed before Maera saw Theo in Nightmare again. Her father once told her that time in Nightmare was different from the Waking World. It could be weeks and even years that go by, but in the Waking World, it might have only been a single hour or as little as a few minutes. That's just how it was.

Secretly, Maera hoped it wouldn't be too long before she saw Theo again, and thankfully, it was only seven days. As she watched Wonders from her window in her room in one of the castle towers, the sky turned from red to purple, transitioning into the night.

To her delight, Theo appeared in the newly created Swamp of Refuse. She hoped he would be properly scared. After all, she had helped make it. Her friends lived there, and naturally, Maera had to see how Theo's nightmare would play out.

She had one problem with making that plan happen.

Bones, the skeleton knight in all his rusted armor, stood guard at her bedroom door. Her father had told Bones to watch her. If she left, Bones would have to go with her, and she knew he wouldn't let her get anywhere near Theo or the new swamp.

"Unless I can ditch him," she murmured. She opened her door to find Bones dutifully guarding her room. "Oh," she blurted. "You're still here."

"The king ordered me to watch you, young Maera," Bones rattled.

Maera smirked. "Of course, and you're doing a good job, Bones, but I'm hungry."

The skeleton dipped his head politely. "Shall I have someone bring up some snail soup? Or worm pasta? Or spider bread?"

"That all sounds so good. Can't *you* go get it?" Maera pressed.

"I'm supposed to watch you," Bones said disapprovingly. "But I can have one of the werewolf guards run to the kitchens and bring some up." The werewolf guards were werewolf-like Wonders who walked on two legs and were furry and tall. They wore only a chest plate of armor and always had a sword at their side. Sometimes, Maera liked to walk down the halls and howl, causing them to instinctively howl a response. It usually irritated them, but she found it funny every time. She wouldn't do that this time. She wanted Bones to leave so she could sneak out.

"Did you still want me to have someone bring you something to eat, young Maera?"

"I guess," she sighed before she shut the door with a pout. She wouldn't be sneaking out with Bones at the door.

"Now what?" she asked herself. She glanced at her bed, and then an idea struck; she smiled. While Bones was busy getting a guard to get her food, she pulled apart her dark purple blankets. Little by little, she tied the ends of each blanket and sheet into a knot, forming a long rope. When she ran out of blankets and pillowcases, she pulled down her curtains to make her rope longer until she felt satisfied. When she was finished, she went to the window and opened it up. She gazed down the tall tower and figured she was at least fifty feet from the ground.

"If only I knew how to fly," she grumbled. She'd seen Theo do it once. She was impressed, and she had spent days afterward, leaping into the air, wishing she could do it too until she finally gave up. Since she couldn't fly, rappelling down her makeshift rope would have to do.

Maera threw the blanket rope out the window, securing an end to her bedpost. She ran back to the window and looked down. Her means for a getaway were just long enough to reach the ground. Carefully, she crawled out the window, gripping the rope with her hands and feet, and she lowered herself to freedom.

When Maera reached the end of the rope, she let go, falling the final few feet and landing hard on the ground.

"That wasn't so bad," she grinned. She took off, racing to the caves at the base of the butte. Smoke tinged the air from the Fire Forest on the other side of the hill, closer to the front of the castle.

When she reached the caves, she hollered, "Bane!" Her voice echoed off the cave wall. She waited, peering into the deep, dark cave. Nothing stirred. Nothing moved. "Bane!" she called out again. "I need you!"

Suddenly, two icy blue eyes snapped open, glowing in the pitch black, and a low, rumbling growl vibrated off the rocks, causing a few to break away from the walls and fall. A heavy foot-step thundered, then another. Soon, a gigantic black bear emerged. His red teeth dripped with spit, and his face bore scars from a creature that had swiped at him with its claws. When Bane was on all fours, he was taller than most men.

"Who dares to wake me from my slumber?" he roared.

"Calm down, Bane. It's just me," Maera announced. Usually, she had a treat to offer him, but since she had to sneak out, she had nothing.

Upon seeing her empty hands, Bane the Bear scowled at her. "I was sleeping," he said grumpily.

"You're always sleeping. Come on. I need you to take me to the Swamp of Refuse."

"Why?" he asked distrustfully, sensing she was up to something.

"I want to inspect it and make sure it doesn't need more Wonders and spooks," Maera shrugged, hoping he would accept her answer.

He glared at her suspiciously.

She sighed. "Consider it as payback for pulling out that huge splinter in your paw a couple of months ago."

"All right!" Bane growled. He exited the cave and lay on his belly, trying to lower himself as much as possible.

Maera had to step on his arm to get a leg high enough to climb onto his back. Once she was adequately seated, he stood. Bane was the tallest and scariest bear in Nightmare, and he was also the fastest. He took off at a brisk pace, racing across the barren Desert of Sorrows. Barreling toward the River of Regret, bits of rock rolled down to the river's edge just as the great bear plunged into the swift-moving water. Bane was so giant that the water level only reached his shoulders at its deepest point.

Maera giggled as he splashed through the gray, murky depths. From there, Bane made their way toward Ghost Town.

Old, abandoned wood and brick buildings silently stood amid sagebrush and a few junipers. The trees had long since lost their needles, leaving them skeletal and gnarled. They creaked whenever the wind blew, adding their voices to the haunted moans that the ghosts made from within. Occasionally, the ghosts dressed in the garb from the time of the Great Wild West reenact a duel with a Sleeper. They would step into the dirt road and shoot off a misty gun, the shot eerily echoing through the town with screams.

In no time, Bane and Maera passed Ghost Town, ignoring the Sleepers along the way. She only cared about observing and watching Theo's nightmare. She hoped that Theo would learn something important from it this time, and then he might wake up with more insight into his waking life. She considered whether his nightmare might reveal what he was struggling with.

Soon, Maera and Bane reached the Swamp of Refuse. A couple of Sleepers wandered and slunk about in their nightmares; they hid and ran from crocodiles that wanted to eat them. Another Sleeper fought while the snakes wrapped around her and squeezed too tightly.

Maera ignored them while Bane splashed through the water and muck. "Okay, Bane, you can drop me off here," she told the large black bear once they were deep in the swampy land. "Thank you for escorting me."

"I should stay and keep an eye on you," Bane growled.

"But wouldn't you rather return to your cozy, dark cave and have a nap?" Maera coaxed.

"Hmmm. That does sound nice," Bane hummed thoughtfully.

"Where it's quiet? I bet you'd feel much better after a nap. Then, you'll be extra scary whenever a Sleeper comes across your cave," Maera pointed out.

"True." Bane considered it, and Maera held her breath. "Fine, but stay out of trouble." Bane turned and galloped out of the swamp. Maera grinned with triumph. She jumped a little with a "Woo hoo!" and then raced to find Theo.

Maera splashed through the swamp; a few times, the mud sucked at her feet to where she nearly tripped. Her purple dress got filthy, but that was okay. When she heard the groans and rasps of the zombies, she quickly trudged into the muddy water of the swamp until it reached her waist, and she hid behind a tree. Just then, she saw Theo running from the zombies. Grunt and Groan closed in on Theo. To her delight, Theo looked good and scared.

"Yes! I knew this nightmare would be a good one," she said to herself.

Suddenly, Theo tripped and fell splat into the mud.

"Hungry," Grunt said with a raspy voice.

"Brains," Groan moaned. The zombies edged closer.

"No! NO! Stop!" Theo crawled away, but he was too slow; the mud sucked at his limbs and kept him from running. Stinky, Fleshy, and Toothless caught up to the scare party, and the zombies surrounded Theo. To Maera's surprise, Theo began to cry. She expected him to scream. Maybe even fight back. She didn't expect him to cry.

"Come on," she whispered. "Do something. Don't just sit there," she urged, but it was useless.

He couldn't hear her and was beyond fear now. He was so terrified that he couldn't move. "Don't take my foot. Please. Please don't," Theo wailed.

His foot? Maera thought. "Why his foot, of all things? I thought zombies only bit people... or sucked out their brains." She crept closer.

"Please, no! Please!" Theo whimpered. "Not my foot."

Maera couldn't understand why his foot was all that important. *Hands, eyes, and even your brain were more important than a foot, right?*

Grunt and Groan reached for Theo. Stinky bared his teeth, ready to bite. Theo trembled in terror, tears running down his face.

"Not my foot," he repeatedly whispered. "Not my foot."

"Why?" Maera asked.

Theo's blue eyes snapped to hers, and she clapped a hand over her mouth. She hadn't meant to ask out loud!

Oh no!

"Maera!" Theo cried. "Maera help. Don't let them take my foot."

Maera backed away; she would seriously get it this time if she were caught interrupting another nightmare.

"Wait! Please. Don't leave me here! Please! Maera. Please don't let them take my foot."

Maera hesitated. She wanted to know why he was so fond of his foot, but if she interfered again, she'd be in big trouble. "Why don't you want them to take your foot?" she questioned, peering at him between Grunt and Toothless.

The zombies paused their pursuit, waiting to see what she'd do, but they didn't back away. Theo was their prey, their prize, and they were supposed to catch him.

"I don't want to be handicapped," he confessed.

"What's... handicapped?" she asked, taking a few steps closer. She'd never heard that word before.

"It means I won't be normal. It means I won't be able to walk right. I'll be different... forever." He slapped at the swampy water as he frowned, splashing Fleshy and Stinky with mud.

"Is that such a bad thing?" Maera inquired.

"Yes!" he screamed. "It's the worst!" He had said it with such anger and despair.

"Okay. Fine. Stinky, Grunt, Groan, Fleshy, and Toothless, don't take his foot." The zombies moaned and grumbled. Satisfied, Maera turned away to leave.

"Wait! You can't leave me here with them!" Theo called out. "They're *zombies*. They'll eat me!"

"Yes, I can," she declared. "I have to. I'm not supposed to interfere with nightmares, remember? You don't even know how much trouble I got into from the last time I helped." She walked away from the scene. "I'm actually not even supposed to be here," she muttered over her shoulder as she turned to glance back at him. "Besides, they're not so bad... once you get to know them!" she hollered, turning away again.

The zombies started their moaning back up; this time, they were louder and closed in on Theo.

"Wait! Please! Please don't leave me here with them! Don't go!" Theo begged.

Maera shouldn't interrupt. He would lose another dream because of it, a good dream.

"Maera! Please!"

"I can't help you, Theo. You have nightmares for a reason! You have to let the nightmare play out! If I interfere again, you'll lose a dream–a good dream!" She shouted as she was walking further away.

"I don't care if I lose a dream! Help me anyway! Please!" Theo called after her, but Maera couldn't do it. Maybe he didn't care now, but he would need those good dreams. Unfortunately, he needed his nightmares, too.

"I can't! I'm sorry, Theo!" Maera took off running and then hid behind a tree to make sure that the nightmare played out.

The zombies already had Theo, but he suddenly shot up into the air.

"What the...," she frowned. "How can he *do* that?" Not many Sleepers could fly in Nightmare. Fear and terror kept them rooted to the spot. That's how nightmares worked. Except Theo had flown for the second time since she'd seen him in Nightmare. Now, he was flying right toward her. He dropped to the ground a couple of feet away and stomped over, splashing her with muddy water.

"You actually left me there," he accused angrily.

"I had to," Maera told him.

"Why?"

"Because my father said so, and he's the King of Nightmares. He said nightmares are important. He said without them, you won't have dreams," she explained.

"But I only ever *have* nightmares," he frowned. "I haven't had a good dream since coming to the hospital."

"Hospital?" Maera tilted her head. They had a hospital in Nightmare called The Crumbling Hospital. It was falling apart and filled with terrifying Wonders who popped out and snatched Sleepers, pulling them into rooms, strapping them onto tables, and scaring them. It had nurses, with only a smile instead of a face, who liked to poke and prod Sleepers with needles. But Theo wasn't having a nightmare of that kind, which was strange. Instead, he was here, worried about his foot getting eaten by zombies.

Sleepers are so strange.

"Yes. That's where sick people go in my world," Theo said.

"You're... sick?" Maera blinked in surprise. He didn't look sick, but then, things weren't always what they seemed in the Land of Dreams.

"Yes," Theo gravely replied. He was just a little taller than she was and appeared healthy enough. He didn't look hungry, like the starving Wonders in Nightmare, where their ribs and bones stuck out beneath their skin. He also didn't look like the sickly, which were the Wonders that had nasty sores and splotches all over them. Some even had black veins.

"You don't look sick," Maera pointed out.

"Well, I am. I have cancer. They found a tumor on my ankle three years ago, which they did surgery on and removed; then, I had to go through chemotherapy. We thought it helped. It had gone away for a while, but then they found it had come back in my foot. This time, it got into my bones, and they said it's now spreading to my leg, so they want to cut it off," Theo said, crossing his arms. However, despite trying to look tough and angry, fear seeped from his eyes in the form of tears. Perhaps that much fear was why he was continuously visiting Nightmare lately.

"Will it fix it?" Maera asked.

Theo exhaled. "What?"

"Will cutting off your leg make you better?"

He scowled at his feet. "The doctor thinks so, but I don't want them to take my leg *or* foot."

"Toothless doesn't have a foot," Maera pointed at the zombies that were slowly creeping toward them. "And Grunt is missing a hand."

"That's different," Theo frowned. "They're zombies. Their bodies are supposed to fall apart because they're *dead*. Their bodies won't hold together if they're dead."

"Oh," Maera said. Theo seemed to know a lot about a lot.

"We should go, they're coming," Theo pointed out. The zombies were splashing closer. Their groans and grunts could be heard now.

Maera shrugged. "So?"

"So? Aren't you scared?"

Maera snorted. "Of them? No. They're my friends."

Theo's mouth fell open in shock. "*They* are your *friends*? How can you be friends with *them*? Don't you have any normal friends?"

"Normal?" Maera blinked rapidly.

"Yes... human."

"They're human," Maera pointed to the zombies with their human-like bodies. Granted, they were falling apart and a little rotten-looking, but still.

"I mean human and *alive*," Theo amended. "You know, like you and me. Normal."

"I'm normal?" Maera blinked, feeling disappointed that Theo considered her that way. "Except I can't be friends with you or any Sleeper," Maera confessed.

"Sleeper?" Theo asked.

"Yes, we Wonders call all of you Sleepers because you can only visit here in your sleep," Maera explained. "You only stay in our realm for a little bit of time while you sleep, then leave as soon as you wake up. We Wonders only interact with Sleepers to scare you, that's it." She didn't tell him that she technically wasn't a Wonder that got to scare, haunt, or hunt Sleepers since she was determined to find her purpose soon. Then she'd finally be like the other Wonders.

"So, you're saying that you don't have any other friends like me?" Theo questioned with astonishment.

"No, and I can't be friends with you either."

"Why not?" Theo asked.

"Because."

"Because why?" Theo pressed while Maera eyed the zombies that were now running toward them.

"Just because," was all she answered before Theo glanced at the zombies and was startled to see how fast they were approaching.

"We should go," Theo said nervously. "I don't want them to catch me." Theo jumped and began floating in the air. "Come on. If we fly, we'll be quicker."

Maera frowned from where she stood in the muddy water. "I can't do that."

"What?"

"Fly."

"Really?" Theo asked with surprise. "Why? It's easy."

She shook her head. "Not for me. I can't fly. I've tried, but I can't do it."

"Want me to teach you?"

Maera felt the world suddenly open up. She would love to learn how to fly.

"I could teach you if you'd like."

"Are you serious?" Maera asked, uncertain.

"Yep! But that means you have to be my friend, and you can't let them get me," he pointed toward the zombies splashing through the muddy water, waiting impatiently for her to decide.

Can I be friends? What if my father found out? "You wouldn't tell anyone, would you?" Maera questioned. "If we become friends, it has to be kept secret."

"I can keep a secret!" Theo declared. "Cross my heart and hope to die." Theo crossed his heart, using his finger to make an X.

"You don't need to go that far," Maera frowned.

Theo laughed. "I won't really die; it's just what you say so that you know I won't break my promise," Theo explained. Then he frowned, noticing that the zombies were pretty close now.

Stinky was in the lead and reached out with his grayish-green hand.

"Maera... hurry. I promise I won't tell anyone that we're friends. Just don't let them catch me."

Can I really be friends with him? She had to admit it sounded fun. She'd never had a friend like Theo before.

"Maera!"

The zombies were nearly upon them, though they struggled a little in the mud.

"Okay," Maera sighed. "Follow me."

She took off, leaving the zombies behind, who looked utterly disappointed. Theo flew after her, dodging and weaving between the branches of trees. They would need to go somewhere where no one would see them, and she knew just the place. She led the way out of the Swamp of Refuse. Keeping to the shadows, she raced toward the Mountains of Terror. If she could get to the spot where the mountains met the Ocean of Despair, she knew of a place where no one ever went, aside from this one old Sleeper from time to time. It was her special spot, but unfortunately, it would take some time to get there on foot. Racing through Nightmare, Maera noticed other Wonders glancing at them curiously. Some gave chase.

"Can't you run any faster?" Theo asked. "We're going to get caught."

"No," Maera huffed. "Not without help." She slowed, feeling a little out of breath. "If I asked any of the Wonders, they'd tell my father, and he won't be happy if he learns that we're hanging out."

"Is there any other way?"

Maera thought for a moment. "I know! There's a special flower that I could eat that makes me run super-fast, but... it's hard to find."

"What does it look like?" Theo asked.

"It's about a foot tall and has black petals that are blood-red at the tips. The stem is dark, dark green. It has purple thorns. Also, the tips of the petals are poky and sharp. It grows on the sides of the mountains."

"I'll go look for some then," Theo said.

"Okay," Maera replied. He zipped through the air, flying faster than she expected, zooming toward the mountains in the distance. Maera started running again, figuring she might as well get a move on and stop standing around.

CHAPTER

FOUR

Theo came back a while later carrying a few Night Fury Flowers. When he gave them to her, she noticed his hands were scratched up from picking the flowers.

"Here," she reached out. "Give me your hands." She set the flowers down while Theo floated closer, holding out his hands. "Now, can you remember what they looked like when they weren't cut up?"

"Yes," Theo replied.

"Good. Close your eyes and think about how they looked before." She brushed her hands over his. "Now open them."

"Whoa! Cool!" Theo looked down to see his hands were all better. "How did you do that?"

"Well, I didn't do much of anything. It was mostly you." She picked up the flowers and pulled off the head and two leaves of one of the flowers. Then, she popped the petals and leaves into her mouth. They were bitter and tasted like copper. She quickly chewed them and swallowed, then pocketed the rest.

"I still think what you did was cool," Theo declared, causing the corners of her lips to turn up.

"Ready?" Maera asked before Theo nodded. "Then follow me!"

She took off, running faster than she ever had, nearly as quickly as Theo was when he flew. They passed through the different parts of Nightmare. She had to eat a couple more flowers whenever the effects faded. She ran and ran while Theo flew just above her. It felt like hours, but they finally reached the rocky shore of the Ocean of Despair. By then, the Night Fury Flower's effects wore off, and Maera was slow again. She picked her way to the craggy mountain cliffsides and began climbing.

"Aren't you scared of falling?" Theo questioned as he hovered nearby.

"No, if I fall and die, I'll just wake up in the castle. You can't really die in Nightmare."

"That's not what my friends say," Theo stated. "My friends say if you die in your dream, you die for real."

"Well, my father says that you can't actually die in a dream, and he's the King of Nightmares, so he would know."

"Does... that mean you've died before?" Theo inquired curiously.

"Only a few times, but it's okay. Sometimes, there are accidents in Nightmare. One time, I accidentally fell off Colossal while flying. Oh, and there was the incident when I accidentally got sucked up in a quicksand pit when I was playing hide and seek with Brigga, the witch. Another time, one of the clowns from the Carnival of Creeps dared me to go to the Desert of Sorrows, and I got swallowed up by a giant worm. It smelled horrible!" Maera reached for the rocks, pulling herself up the side of the cliff. "Each time, I woke up in my room."

"I'm scared of dying," Theo confessed.

"I'm not. Not here."

"I mean, dying for real," Theo explained. "Not in a dream or nightmare."

"What happens if you die for real?" Maera asked as she climbed even higher up the sheer cliffside while Theo hovered close by.

"I don't know. I think you go to Heaven or something," Theo said with a furrowed brow, looking uncertain.

"Is that bad?" Maera questioned.

"I don't think so."

"Then why are you scared?" Maera exhaled as she pulled herself up another couple of feet.

"Because I'm too *little* to die, and I don't want to leave my parents or friends. I know my parents would be very sad if I did, so I don't want to. Plus, I'm scared that it might hurt."

"Oh. I guess then I don't want to die for real either."

"I'm also worried that... well... what if I end up somewhere I don't like? What if it's like coming here?" Theo questioned.

"It won't be. Sleepers don't stay here," Maera answered breathily. "You must be born from the Sand of Imagination to live here. That's where all the Wonders come from and all the dreams and nightmares, too."

"You're born from sand?" Theo floated higher as Maera continued to climb further up the cliff.

"I live here, don't I?" Maera shot back as if it were obvious. Suddenly, the rock she reached for crumbled and fell, causing Maera to slip.

"Careful!" Theo called out as she swung, hanging by her right hand. He quickly flew over and pulled her left hand up to the next rock sticking out. "Hold on to this!" She grabbed it, but he continued to hold onto her until he was certain she was stable. Maera laughed.

"What's so funny?" Theo demanded, letting her go.

He sounds so worried! Maera's grin widened. "Did I *scare* you?"

"Yes! I really thought you were going to fall!"

"I've never scared anyone before." When Maera was certain

she wouldn't slip again, she resumed climbing up the steep cliff-side nearly halfway.

"I thought you lived here. Doesn't that mean you're supposed to scare people like me?"

"I suppose," Maera said before grabbing another rock and pulling herself even higher.

"You don't usually scare Sleepers then?"

"No," Maera flushed pink.

"Why not?"

"That's what I'm hoping to figure out," she grunted, getting a better foothold and pushing herself up a few more feet. "Whenever someone is born here, they find their purpose and do the job they were born to do," she explained before pulling herself up to another rock jutting out. "I never found mine, so I never joined the others in scaring Sleepers." Finally, with one final heave, Maera reached the top, hauling herself up and over the ledge. She collapsed for a moment, feeling winded. Laying there, she looked up at the starry sky until Theo blocked her view.

"So, you don't have a purpose?" Theo landed and sat beside her.

"I do. I just have to find it," Maera replied, "but I never scared anyone before."

"Well, you scared me. I seriously thought you were going to fall and die," Theo mumbled.

"Like I said, I won't actually die here. I would just wake up in my room in the castle," Maera laughed.

"And then I'd be here all alone," Theo complained. Suddenly, a flurry of bats swooped into the sky from the dark cracks and crevices in the mountain above them. Their chittering and sporadic flight pattern caused Maera to smile and Theo to frown.

Maera glanced at him as the bats disappeared into the night. "Are you afraid of being alone?"

"Here? Definitely. This place gives me the creeps," he shuddered, eyeing some dark crevices suspiciously. "There are so many scary things everywhere."

"They're only nightmares, Theo," Maera said, sitting up. Her feet dangled over the edge.

"Exactly." He drew his knees in and looked out at the world beyond. "What's out there?" He pointed toward the ocean.

"I don't know. I never go out that far from home," Maera confessed. "I've heard there are pirates."

"Do you think there are sea monsters?" Theo asked, looking a little afraid at the idea of it.

"Most likely," Maera shrugged.

"That's creepy. Does anyone drown?"

"Oh yes," Maera replied. "That's part of Nightmare. Sometimes, I hear stories about the nightmares that happen on the ocean. One day, I hope to see one."

Theo frowned. "You want to *watch* someone drown?"

"No!" She shook her head. "That's boring. Once a Sleeper drowns, they either start breathing underwater and continue the nightmare or wake up and disappear. No, I want to see pirates and other Wonders that exist out there. I hear wild storms sometimes blow in and toss ships around, or the ocean swirls, creating a whirlpool that sucks ships down to the sandy depths below."

"Why would you want to see that?" Theo asked.

"Why wouldn't I?" she questioned, realizing Theo didn't find Nightmare to be as wondrous as she did. "I suppose I want to find out if the nightmares on the ocean are scarier than the ones on land. Besides, seeing what Sleepers do in their nightmares is always interesting; sometimes, crazy things happen."

"Like what?"

"Like flying," Maera answered.

"Not many people here can fly?"

"Not in their nightmares, no," Maera replied.

"Is that why you can't?" Theo asked.

"I live here, remember? I'm not a part of the nightmares. Not until I find my purpose. So, that's not why. I just... can't fly. Only certain Wonders in Nightmare can. Witches, shadow monsters, ghosts, dragons, killer crows, and other winged creatures can fly. Though, I suppose the witches, ghosts, and shadow monsters float, not fly."

"I see. Maybe you can fly, but you don't know it yet," Theo offered.

"You said you could teach me?"

"Sure! Let's go!" Theo got up and backed away from the ledge, looking a little green when he glanced down. Maera stood and followed him with a smile.

Theo gets scared so easily!

The ledge they walked along led to a cave that was the halfway point on the mountain. Theo stopped while Maera skipped on past him, heading right toward the dark crevice. Cool, musty air drifted by the closer they got.

"Are we going... in there?" Theo pointed with a shaky finger at the dark entrance. The wind howled through the cave, making it groan and adding a spooky effect.

"Yep! Come on!" Maera ran into the gloomy cavern, and Theo had no choice but to follow. Inside, she hummed a haunting tune.

Theo chewed on his lip. "Why are you humming such a scary-sounding song?"

"It's not scary to me," Maera answered. "I think it's pretty." She started humming again, and Theo quietly followed her. Soon, they saw a light up ahead. "Hurry! I think you're going to like this."

Maera picked up her pace toward the opening, and Theo hurried after her. The cave eventually opened to reveal a small valley on the other side. Black Pegasusses with purple eyes flew overhead like shadows against the patches of starry sky. The flying horses looked majestic as they soared above, and their manes and tails were blue flames instead of horsehair. Below, black, skeletal unicorns munched on blue-green grass. A glowing green waterfall cascaded over the far cliff, dumping into the winding, murky river that snaked through the valley. Rabbits with coarse, gray fur, sharp yellow teeth, and bright red eyes hopped around.

"Isn't it beautiful?" Maera asked with a big smile, spreading out her arms and spinning in a circle.

"It's... something," Theo replied, though he didn't look so sure about it.

"Don't be such a scaredy cat!" Maera laughed. "Come down here. I want you to meet my friends! They never tell on me. Hardly anyone comes here anymore; it took me ages to discover it!" Maera raced down the narrow rocky path toward the grassy lands below. A few dark blue flowers stuck out here and there from the tops of the long grass that swished in the light breeze. Theo jumped off the ledge, flying to the ground. When he landed, Maera took his hand, leading him to meet one of the skeletal unicorns.

"This is Dreary. She was born several years ago. I always wondered where she'd gone until I stumbled across that cave and came here." Maera petted Dreary's tangled, stringy mane. Her sharp, silver horn glinted in the moonlight as she bowed her head, and Maera moved closer to stroke her bony nose. "Want to pet her?"

"I don't know," Theo said, looking suspicious and unsure of the creature.

"It's okay, she won't gut you... not if I tell her not to," Maera promised, then turned toward the unicorn. "Dreary, don't stab Theo with your horn." Dreary tossed her head in a nod. "See?" Maera smiled. Theo was now eyeing the sharp horn with wariness, looking scared again. Maera rolled her eyes. "Come *on*," she bossed. Taking Theo's hand, she pulled him closer and placed it on Dreary's mane.

"It feels... tangly and... a little greasy," Theo grimaced.

"Pet her nose–she likes that," Maera instructed. Theo carefully petted the unicorn's bony, black nose until the mare snorted, startling Theo and causing Maera to laugh.

"What's so funny?" Theo grumbled.

"You are so silly! She's not going to *bite*," Maera giggled. "You're such a scaredy cat."

"Am not," Theo argued. He gave Dreary one last pet to prove he wasn't afraid before they moved on. Maera picked up one of the hissing rabbits, flashing its sharp teeth, handing it to Theo. It was brown, and the fur was so bristly it poked out in all directions, which she thought was cute.

"This is Rabies," she told him. "You can pet him. Oh, and this is Feral. She's a girl," Maera said, picking up the other hissing rabbit. She stroked her gray, wiry fur a couple of times, then set Feral down. Theo just as quickly set Rabies down, not daring to pet any of the rabbits.

"Don't you want to learn how to fly?" he questioned before she could introduce him to any more of her friends.

"Oh yeah! We probably should before you wake up and disappear," Maera said logically. "There's a good place to practice!" She pointed to the flat grassy area near the widest bend in the green river.

"That works."

"Now what?" Maera asked.

"Now, imagine yourself lifting into the air and being weightless. Imagine your body being light as a feather, and spread your arms like an airplane."

"Light as a feather," Maera repeated, then spread her arms. "Light as a feather," she said again, then jumped. Two seconds later, she landed with a thump and frowned. "It didn't work."

Theo shook his head and smiled. "You have to actually believe that you can fly. This is a dream, after all. You can do it if you think you can. Oh, and lean forward. You should float before you hit the ground. But you won't if you have doubts or don't think you can. Try again and believe that you are so light that you can't help but float. Imagine the wind carrying you up higher and higher."

"Okay. I'll try." Maera tried leaning forward with her arms out and face-planted on the ground. "Ouch!" She got back up and rubbed her forehead. "That didn't work either."

"Try again. See yourself flying. Picture it and then do it."

The only way she could picture flying was by how the birds flew. So she closed her eyes and pretended she was a feather, floating in the air, letting the wind pick her up and take her higher.

At first, nothing happened, and then she felt it... just the tiniest of shifts. Something tickled her between the shoulder blades on her back. For a moment, she felt weightless, light as air, and her feet rose off the ground. She opened her eyes to see if she was doing it, but in doing so, she lost her concentration and dropped back to the ground. Still, she'd done it!

"I did it! I did it! You saw, right? For a second? I floated!"

Theo grinned. "Oh, I didn't see, but that's great. Now, see if you can do it for longer."

Maera tried again, imagining herself as light as a feather, light as air. Sadly, it felt more challenging this time. She tried flapping her arms like she'd seen the birds and dragons do until Theo was laughing so hard she lost concentration.

She scowled. "What's so funny?"

"Why are you flapping your arms?" Theo snickered.

"Because! That's what birds and dragons do!" Maera huffed.

"They flap their wings to fly. You don't have wings, so you

shouldn't need to flap your arms to do it. Look, I don't flap *my* arms, and *I* can still fly."

Maera studied him as he hovered in the air. "Hmmm." She felt silly now.

"Whatever you did the first time, do it again. Be lighter than air and let the wind lift you," Theo told her. She closed her eyes.

"Let the wind lift me," she repeated. "Be like a feather, light as a feather," she chanted. Imagining her body as weightless, she tried to let the wind pick her up. Her back tingled between her shoulder blades. The tingling grew stronger until, with one big *woosh*, Maera was airborne.

"Whoa! You have wings?!" Theo asked with amazement. Maera opened her eyes, realizing that what felt like her muscles twitching were silver wings.

"I have wings!" Maera shouted as they flapped behind her. However, the moment she noticed this and recalled not having wings, they disappeared, and she fell to the ground. Landing on her back, the air pushed out of her, and she couldn't breathe for a second.

"Maera! Are you okay?" Theo dropped down and ran over to help her up. Maera then sucked in a fresh breath of air.

"I'm fine," she wheezed. "I guess I need to work on that."

"Yes, and...." His voice trailed off as his face scrunched into a frown.

"What's wrong?"

Theo's eyes grew bigger. "I—I—I—I'm waking up! I don't want to go back to the hospital. Don't let the doctor take me, Maera!" Theo panicked, reaching toward her. "If I wake up, they're going to cut off my foot. I don't want the doctor to take my foot!"

Maera tried to grab his hand.

"Theo! I can't reach you!" Except Theo didn't get any closer.

He hung in the air as if he were trapped; tears fell down his face as he tried desperately to reach for her. Maera tried jumping, but she still couldn't reach him.

"Use your wings, Maera, please! I don't want to go back."

"Theo, I'm trying!" She tried jumping higher, but suddenly, Theo disappeared. She landed with a thump, skidding on a couple of loose rocks before she got her footing.

"He woke up." Maera kicked at a larger rock, disappointed that he was gone. He was different from all the Wonders she knew in Nightmare. She never realized just how interesting Sleepers were until she met Theo. Sadly, Sleepers never stayed for too long. They always woke up eventually.

"But he'll be back, I'm sure," she thought out loud while she tapped her chin with her finger. "And when he does come back, I'll show him I can fly." The surrounding Wonders watched Maera curiously while she practiced sprouting wings and flying. Some of the flying horses whinnied at her whenever she fell as if they found it funny. Eventually, Maera remained airborne for a solid ten minutes, flying higher and higher.

"Look! I'm doing it!" Maera exclaimed with glee as she flew past the tops of the mountains. As she practiced, she caught a glimpse of the familiar old man whom she sometimes saw in this special spot. He looked up at her, and she waved. He was the only Sleeper who came to this place. She was so excited to show someone her new ability. He smiled as she zipped through the air.

Flying is AWESOME! "Woohoo! This is so much better than walking on the ground."

Unfortunately, the moment she thought of the ground and about walking, her wings disappeared, and she fell. The elderly man looked concerned as she plummeted to the ground, and he reached out his hand from where he stood at the entrance of the cave; however, he was too far. She tried thinking about being light as a feather, but despite coaxing her wings back into existence, they wouldn't return.

"Darn!" Maera said. Just then, she hit the ground, blacked out, and disappeared.

CHAPTER

FIVE

Maera woke up in her bedroom inside the black castle, and for a moment, she debated sneaking out to look for Theo. Maybe he'd have a nightmare about the hospital. She could find him more easily if he did. Sitting up, Maera rubbed her eyes. Sadly, she noticed Alessandra sitting in the corner of her room, waiting for her to wake up. The vampire didn't look happy. Well, she never looked happy, but she seemed grumpier than usual today. Her glowing red eyes were narrowed in a frown.

"Your father wants to talk to you," the vampire said, her sharp fangs standing out in the dark shadows of her room. "He's been waiting for hours."

Maera groaned, not looking forward to the coming reprimand. The rope of blankets sat on the floor in the moonlight, shining through the window. Maera was in trouble... again. The vampire stood, her long black hair hanging down her back like a sheet. Her skin was so pale that it was nearly white, making her red eyes stand out even more.

"Hurry, I don't have all day," Alessandra hissed. "I'm to get you cleaned up and then take you to your father. You're absolutely filthy! What did you do? Bathe in the bog?"

Maera frowned down at her muddy dress before Alessandra stalked over and grabbed Maera's arm with an icy cold hand. Alessandra's long nails bit into Maera's skin as she pulled her toward the washroom.

A LITTLE WHILE LATER, Maera was cleaned up and wearing a dark blue dress. Alessandra had brushed her tangled hair and pulled it up into braids that she clipped around Maera's head like a crown. When she finished, Maera followed Alessandra out of her room, shutting the door, which had the number "3 1 1" carved into it for no reason she knew of. They wound their way through the castle until they reached the dining hall. Inside, Maera was surprised that only her father sat at the large table. All his royal subjects in Nightmare were absent.

"Maera, come in. I wanted to speak with you alone," his voice boomed. "Alessandra, you're dismissed." The vampire scurried off, leaving Maera alone with her father. "Come," he ordered. Maera sat in the seat next to him where piles of putrid food were laid out. She waited, unsure if she should dish a plate after the lecture or before.

"Go ahead and fill your plate. We'll talk over our breakfast," the king said.

Maera scooped out some ant pudding, then grabbed a beetle roll. Next, she scooped a few roasted cockroaches out and sprinkled them with some sulfur salt before she ate. The castle served the best food in all of Nightmare, and it was perfectly awful. She prided herself on the fact that she ate only the *worst* food Nightmare had to offer, something not all Wonders got to do.

"Maera, I have to say, I'm a little disappointed with you. Bones told me you had snuck out after I told him to watch you. Why? Why did you do that?" the king questioned.

"I...," Maera swallowed her food and then dropped her eyes down to her plate. "I wanted to see the new nightmare. I noticed a few Sleepers were there."

"You could have gone there with Bones. Why did you sneak off?" he demanded.

Maera shrugged. "I don't know."

"Is it because you interrupted another nightmare?" he asked. Maera turned. Her father's face was one of disappointment. His silver eyes watched her closely while he waited for her to answer. When she didn't, he sighed.

"Maera, I told you not to do that. Grunt and Groan said they lost their charge and couldn't finish the nightmare shortly after you appeared."

"But I didn't stop the nightmare, Father. I only had a question for the Sleeper. When he answered the question, I left. He freed himself. He can *fly,* Father."

"He may have saved himself, but it was only *after* you got involved. You mustn't interfere, Maera. That could change *every-thing.* Are you prepared to face the consequences if things do change because of it?" His sharp tone caused Maera to frown.

"I guess not," she pouted. "I only wanted to see the new nightmare."

"And that was yesterday morning. You were gone all day, so where were you after that?" the king probed.

"I just went to check on a couple of other nightmares." Technically, that was true.

"I don't like you wandering off by yourself," her father said in a serious tone. "Parts of this land are disappearing. In the Waking

World, Sleepers have invented distractions—devices that steal away their attention—inventions that numb them and clog their minds until they no longer imagine new things or create new dreams of their own. Our world... it's growing smaller. Sleepers don't sleep as long as they once did. They're distracted and busier."

Maera poked at her food. "What does that mean?"

"It means they have fewer ideas and inventions. They watch more *television*, play more games, and use these things called *phones* and *tablets*. They observe other people's inventions and ideas without creating their own. The dreams they do have are the ones that others have already shaped. Parts of our world are disappearing because of it. I don't want to lose you, my daughter. If you're stuck in a place that's disappearing...." He didn't finish.

"I won't go to any of the forgotten nightmares. I only ever go to the places Sleepers visit," she assured him.

"I see, well, next time, I want you to take someone with you."

"Do I have to?" Maera whined. "I know where to go and where not to go. I don't need someone to babysit me."

"Until you show me that you can be responsible, I don't want you out there on your own," he replied sternly.

"But I wasn't alone," Maera blurted before she could help it.

The king's eyes narrowed. "Who was with you?"

"Just some skeletal unicorns, Father," she answered. *That was close.*

"Where?"

"By the Terror Mountains," she replied.

"Maera, the area nearest the Ocean of Despair, is on the edge of the forgotten lands. It borders Dream, so steer clear of that."

"Okay, Father. I will." She spooned out the baked fish eyeballs with moldy cheese sauce melted over the top, dipping her beetle roll in it before eating it up. It was the perfect blend of doughy fluff with a bit of crunch. The cheese sauce only enhanced the flavor.

"So, what were you doing all day yesterday? And why did I feel you die?" he questioned with concern.

"Oh, um, well...." Maera considered how much she could tell him. "I, um, sort of learned that I could fly. Only, I'm not really good at it yet."

The King of Nightmares paused his eating of mashed worms in gravy and stared at her. "Really?" He didn't look entirely happy. If she didn't know any better, she'd say he looked a little sad.

"Is that... bad?"

"No," he said slowly. "It just means that you're becoming more aware of yourself. I believe it to be a good thing, though. How did you do it?" he asked, but his tone was much more friendly this time.

"I discovered I have wings!" Maera exclaimed with excitement.

"Wings? You have wings?" He crossed his arms and then leaned back, tapping his lip with his forefinger.

"Yes. Silver ones," Maera said with a big smile. "What kind of nightmare Wonder has those?"

"None," the king answered. "Maybe after this, you can show me," he suggested, and Maera smiled.

"Okay!" She thought for a moment. "Do you think I'll be able to find my purpose now?" Maera asked with newfound hope.

"I think...," he paused with consideration, "you're getting closer. How did you figure it out?"

"Oh, um... I think I saw one of the Sleepers doing it, so I thought I'd give it a try."

"You're such a smart girl," her father said with a proud smile.

"But why do you think I grew wings?" she asked. "Do other Wonders change when they're here a long time?"

"Not often. Usually, when one Wonder is no longer needed, it disappears just like the land disappears when Sleepers stop dreaming certain dreams. Then new ones are born," her father answered. "However, sometimes, in rare cases, a Sleeper can change parts of a dream or nightmare. Those Sleepers are rare and have a much stronger imagination."

"Oh." Maera pondered if Theo could. She hadn't seen it happen before, but that didn't mean that he couldn't.

AFTER EATING, Maera and the king walked the halls until they reached the doors leading to the courtyard. Outside, blood-red roses bloomed on black thorny stems. Purple and black ones grew on dark-green thorny vines. A black fountain in the center spouted red water. Butterflies with skeletal white wings fluttered from flower to flower. Their lacy wings were delicate and glowed softly. Some Sleepers thought they looked scary, but Maera always thought they were beautiful. She always thought being a little different was a good thing.

"So," her father cleared his throat, capturing her attention. "I thought you were going to show me your wings."

"That's right!" Smiling, Maera concentrated hard. Focusing on becoming light and weightless, she waited until her back tingled and she felt her silver wings sprout. Then, in a woosh, she pushed off the ground, flapping her wings and levitating a few feet higher from the ground.

"Marvelous, daughter, how wonderful! What a brilliant discovery." The king looked impressed, and Maera beamed. Then, feeling daring, she flapped her wings harder and rose *higher* into the air, then she swooped a little, dipping lower before she landed on the ground in front of her father.

"I don't want to go too high," she declared, smoothing out her dress. "Last time, I fell and woke up here."

"Ah, so that's how you died. You are wise to be more careful. Still, I think it's amazing that you can fly. You're such a special girl." They remained in the courtyard garden for a little longer. Her father walked on the stony paths while Maera showed off her newfound flying skills.

That night, the King of Nightmares invited Maera back to the throne room and to the giant hourglass. The king had interrupted her daydreaming about finding Theo in the hospital. She wondered what happened to people's limbs when the doctors took them away; perhaps there were piles of them somewhere that only doctors knew about. She never saw a doctor, but that was who Theo said would take his foot.

Alessandra escorted Maera to the throne room, and Maera raced up the stairs to the balcony. This time, the nobles gathered around below to watch.

"Look," her father pointed with his staff. "What do you see?"

"More sand!" Maera grinned with delight. "Lots more!" The pile in the bottom was higher than the last time she'd seen it.

"Want to see a new nightmare be born?" the king offered.

"Can I?" Maera clapped with a bounce of excitement.

"Yes. What about you, my people? Shall I create a new nightmare?" he asked the nobles below, and they all cheered. "Very well." Her father tapped on the glass base of the hourglass, and sand rose, turning into red light and getting sucked up into the staff. Lots of sand did this until his staff was glowing brighter than ever before. After making the large, round, stained-glass window disappear, the king faced the world beyond. Casting his staff out, a red light burst from the end toward the Crumbling Hospital.

"What did you do?" Maera asked.

"I created a new addition to the hospital nightmare."

The king tapped his staff against the hourglass again, collecting more red light from the sand. Then he thumped the bottom of the staff on the ground three times, and the light burst outward. Suddenly, a man stood before them in a white coat, looking almost like a Sleeper, but he didn't quite look like any Sleeper she'd ever seen. He had black eyes, and when he smiled, it split his face in half because his smile was so large, bigger than any Sleeper's. He hovered and was surrounded by a circle of red light. The king floated him through the air, using his staff so that everyone below could see. The nobles clapped their hands, and the new Wonder's smile became impossibly bigger. Her father magically brought him closer to the window.

Maera laughed at the Wonder's goofy smile. "Your smile is surely going to scare someone. You look so funny!" The Wonder frowned. "Oh! Not that they'll laugh at you. Sleepers will *definitely* be scared of you," she assured him, and the man smiled again with that crazy, overly wide smile.

"What is he?" she asked her father. He looked familiar, like she'd seen something like him before, but she couldn't say where. She'd seen nurse Wonders, who were perfectly creepy, but no one like this.

"A doctor... or at least, he represents the nightmare version of one," her father said. "Have you been thinking of doctors or hospitals lately?"

"Actually, I have," Maera's brows drew together in thought. "That's weird! I was thinking of hospitals all morning, and now there's a doctor Wonder!"

"Yes," her father replied. "What a funny coincidence." Yet he didn't seem all that surprised by it.

"What does that mean?" she inquired.

"I'm sure it's nothing, though I think someone is about to have a nightmare about a doctor. I can feel it coming. I need to send this Wonder to the hospital right away."

"Oooh! I'll call him Doc, then," Maera decided.

"A good name," her father smiled, and he sent Doc in the direction of the new nightmare. "When will the nightmare happen?"

"It's going to happen very soon," her father answered.

"Can I watch? Please?"

"I don't think that's a good idea. You've been interfering with the nightmares quite a bit lately," the king frowned. "I can't have you messing with any others."

"I'll take someone with me this time!" Maera promised.

The king studied her for a long moment, then sighed. "I suppose a glance won't do any harm," he said. Her heart lifted. "But don't interrupt the nightmare," he warned. "Do you hear me? You'll take Alessandra with you."

Maera's heart sank. Alessandra was no fun. She was such a crab. "But-"

"You either go with her or not at all," her father replied firmly.

"Fine," Maera grumbled, drawing the word out. They turned from the open window, and the king magicked the stained glass back into place. Looking out over the balcony, he tapped his staff, and the nobles parted.

"Guards! Send for Alessandra." Two werewolves in armor left to retrieve the vampire. By the time the king and his daughter descended the stairs, the skinny vampire had walked through the doors in her dark maroon dress. The other nobles had left to talk or do whatever fancy nobles did in castles.

"My king?" Alessandra curtsied.

"You will escort Princess Maera to the new nightmare. Make sure she doesn't interfere, though," the king ordered.

"Very well," Alessandra slid her glowing red eyes toward Maera, who smiled at the vampire, hoping Alessandra wouldn't be as crabby as usual. "Come," the vampire beckoned.

Maera skipped down the platform steps to meet her.

Vampires had a special ability to blend into the shadows and appear in new places. Maera's father could also do that.

Maera took Alessandra's outstretched hand, and she pulled Maera into a dark corner of the throne room toward the shadows. One second, they were in the castle, and the next, they were inside the hallway of the Crumbling Hospital. They passed other Sleepers having various nightmares. Alessandra used her abilities to hide Maera and herself in the shadows so they didn't interfere with the Sleepers.

When Maera spotted Doc, she gasped with excitement. "There! There's Doc!"

"Shush," Alessandra hissed. "I can hide us in shadows, but that does nothing to silence your voice."

"Right," Maera muttered. "He's going somewhere. We should follow!"

"Lower your voice, Princess," Alessandra chided impatiently.

Maera ducked her head. "Sorry."

Sneaking through the hall, they followed Doc until he entered a room marked 310. Maera tugged on Alessandra's hand toward the room, and they positioned themselves outside. On the other side of the door, she heard someone yell.

"No, wait! Stop! I shouldn't be awake for this! Where's my mom? Mom? Mom! Mom! I'm not asleep, and they're going to take my leg! Mom! I'm not sleeping yet! Mom! Help!"

Maera peaked through the door's window to get a better look. Whoever was inside didn't even realize they were actually sleeping and having a nightmare.

"Mom! Help! No!" That voice... it sounded like Theo.

"Theo?" she inquired with a frown, standing on her tippy toes to get a better look. To Maera's surprise, the boy inside was Theo. "It is!"

"I said hush!" Alessandra hissed, but it was too late. Theo glanced past the scary doctor and instantly spotted Maera; his eyes were wide with fear. He was increasingly startled when he noticed Alessandra standing next to Maera. Maera was sure that her glowing red eyes caused the terror. Sadly, this ruined Doc's hunt, and Doc stood still; he was confused and no longer the leading character in the nightmare.

"This is a nightmare," Theo murmured, putting it together.

"Now look what you've done!" Alessandra snapped, yanking Maera from the doorway and toward the shadows.

"No! Wait! Wait! Come back! Maera!" Theo called out.

Before Alessandra could get Maera into the shadows, Theo burst through the door, running in some strange sort of hospital gown. The confused Doc followed him.

"Maera, hurry up! Your father will not be happy about this at all," Alessandra lectured, yanking Maera away from Theo's room. Theo reached his hand toward them, but Alessandra pulled Maera further down the hall away from him and Doc.

"Theo! I'm sorry!" Maera shouted back at Theo.

Alessandra was almost to the shadows.

"She's going to pull me into the shadows, and then I won't be here anymore," Maera said helplessly.

"No! Wait!"

Like many nightmares, no matter how fast Theo ran, his progress slowed, and Doc got closer. Theo glanced behind him and panicked when he saw Doc gaining on him. Theo looked back at Maera with desperation. "Maera! He's going to take my leg! Help me!"

"I really can't this time, I'm sorry!" Maera hollered while Alessandra tugged harder, dragging her toward the shadows.

Theo still couldn't outrun Doc, and he was growing more afraid.

"No, no, no!" he screamed.

Maera didn't like how upset he was, but she couldn't help, not again.

Unless... Maera suddenly had an idea. She jerked out of Alessandra's grasp. "Theo!" He looked at her with such hope. "*I* can't help," she told him. "But *you* can! You can change the nightmare! Use your imagination and change the dream!"

"Hush!" Alessandra scolded, grabbing her arm and pulling her away. "You've caused enough trouble. Now hurry up, we're leaving."

Doc had finally caught up to Theo, and Maera watched from a distance. Unfortunately, Maera couldn't escape Alessandra. Theo was on his own this time. She watched Doc grab Theo while Alessandra pulled her down the hall.

"No!" Theo shrieked with despair while the doctor hauled him back to the room. "Stop! No! No! Don't take me back there! Not in there! No! I'm not ready! I'm not ready! Maera!"

Maera felt like her heart was being squeezed, and she wished there was more she could do. Theo screamed, and it was painful to hear and see the terror her new friend was experiencing. If only *she* could teach Theo how to face his fears. If only *she* could teach him to be brave. Sometimes, having someone there with you was the best way to get through the hard stuff. She'd face the nightmare with him if it weren't for Alessandra.

Too bad Theo can't turn the shadows into a puddle of black tar. Then Alessandra would be stuck and unable to take me back to the castle. Then I could stay.

"What the heck?" Alessandra questioned in alarm.

To Maera's surprise, the shadows suddenly sucked Alessandra's feet up. No, not shadows. Black goo! Tar!

"What have you *done*?" Alessandra wailed.

"Me?" Maera blinked. "How could *I* do this? I'm not a Sleeper." Only Sleepers and the king could influence Nightmare.

Did Theo listen to my advice? Was he changing the dream?

"You did this somehow! I know you did!" Alessandra snarled while she sank, the black tar reaching her knees.

"I'm sorry! I really don't know how that happened." Distracted, Alessandra let go of Maera's hand. "Get me out of this!" Alessandra demanded.

"I don't know how!" Maera looked around. There was nothing that she could use to help the vampire. "Don't wiggle. You'll only sink faster."

Alessandra stopped moving, and she remained at the same depth, no longer sinking into the black tar.

A scream pulled at Maera's attention. This was her chance. "Sorry, I have to go," she said, leaving Alessandra to help Theo.

"Wait! Don't leave me here! Maera! Get back here right now! MAERA!" Alessandra screeched, but Maera ran toward the other person who was screaming, the one who *actually* needed her.

CHAPTER

SIX

The moment Maera returned to Theo's room, she was horrified when she looked through the little window in the door and saw she was too late. Doc was holding a doll's foot; Theo's nightmare had come true. Although, why his foot had turned into a doll's foot, she didn't know. When she burst into the room, Doc dropped the foot in surprise, and she watched as the foot hopped up and down.

"My foot!" Theo cried. Where his foot once was, there was only a stub.

"It's okay," Maera assured him. "It's not that bad."

Tears ran down Theo's face in streams. "It's *not* okay. It's never going to *be* okay ever again!"

"Maybe we can put it back on," Maera shrugged.

Through misty, wet eyes, Maera saw a spark of hope ignite within him... until he glanced at Doc, who grinned that large, face-splitting crazy smile.

Theo's hope seemed to dim. "But what about him?" he asked.

"Him? He's just happy because you're his first Sleeper. He was born earlier today. Oh, and he's happy that he took your foot." Maera turned to Doc. "Good job, Doc, you can go now."

Doc nodded, his grin spreading wider over his face.

Theo shivered.

The only sound left in the room was the *tap, tap, tap* of the doll's foot as it hopped around the room.

"Come on!" Maera said when she saw the foot hopping out the door after Doc. It slipped through just before it closed. "Let's go after that foot!"

Theo got out of bed, and Maera helped him hobble toward the door. When they opened it, Doc was gone, but the plastic foot bounced up and down at the end of the hall.

"There!" Maera pointed. Together, they hurried after it. Theo had to hop the whole way. "Can you fly?" she asked. They'd never catch up to the wayward appendage if they kept their current pace.

"Uh, I think so. Earlier, I was too scared." Theo gave it a try, and quickly, he was floating. "I can fly again!"

Maera smiled and then ran. "Come on! Let's go! Before it gets away!" They chased after his foot, running past Alessandra, who was still stuck in black tar, admiring her long, glossy fingernails. She looked annoyed as they ran past her.

"Hey! Get back here, Maera, and get me out of this!" Alessandra barked. "Don't you dare leave me here! I swear I will bite you in your sleep if you don't get me out of here this instant!"

Maera ignored the vampire.

"What happened to *her*?" Theo asked.

Maera frowned as they raced after the foot. "I thought *you* did that."

"I didn't do it. What is that stuff?"

"Well, one moment it was a shadow, then the next, a puddle of black goo, and she got stuck. If she hadn't, I would've been long gone by now. Vampires can travel through shadows, you know. That's how we got here so fast from the castle."

Theo looked around just as they rounded a corner. "Dang! Where did my foot go?"

Maera looked to see that the foot had indeed disappeared. They ventured down the hall and came across the elevators. The lights showed the elevator going down. "How did it get in there?"

"I don't know, but we need to go after it!" Theo said. "Look, I think there are stairs through those doors!"

She ran to the stairs while Theo flew after her. When they reached the bottom, they made it to the elevator doors just as they were closing. They spotted the runaway foot hopping straight for the hospital's exit.

"Over there!" Theo yelled. Maera took off as Theo zipped after it, blasting through the doors to the outside. The foot hopped around the side of the building, and they hurried after it.

"Oh no," Theo groaned with despair when they rounded the corner of the building to find mountains of doll arms, legs, hands, and feet. "How are we ever going to find it now?" Theo questioned hopelessly.

"I'm not sure," Maera panted. "This is all new." She frowned at what her father had created. "Can you fly higher and check for movement?"

"I'll try," Theo answered before he shot into the air, going higher while Maera tried to summon her wings. Once her wings spread out, Maera caught up to Theo, and her frown soon matched his. There were many doll hands, feet, and other limbs that all wiggled and hopped toward various piles of appendages. It looked like a garbage heap of doll parts.

"There's no way I'll find it now—not with so many to sort through! It's... *gone*. It's really gone," he stammered, choking down a sob.

They dropped to the ground, where Theo sat in the dirt, pulled up his knees, and cried.

"It's okay, Theo, don't cry," Maera said softly.

"Can you fix it?" Theo sniffled. "Like how you fixed my hands?"

"I could try." She sat down next to him. "All right, close your eyes."

Theo closed his eyes.

"Good," Maera nodded. "Now picture having your foot back. Picture it being whole." She ran her hand over where his foot once was, but this time, nothing happened. She tried a second time.

"Did it work?" Theo asked, but when he looked, he saw it hadn't. "Why won't it work?"

"I don't know. Are you picturing it being whole again?"

"I—I...," he frowned. "I can't." Tears filled his eyes once more. "It feels like it's gone... for good." He put his head back down over his arms, his shoulders shaking as he sobbed.

"It's okay," Maera said quickly, rubbing his back. "I think you look more handsome now."

"What?" Theo glanced up at her with puffy red eyes.

"You look better than you did before," Maera confessed and then smiled. "In fact, now you fit right in. You look like you could be one of us!"

Theo's face fell. "I look *scary*?"

"Yes! Isn't it *wonderful*?" Maera responded brightly.

Theo looked around at the various doll parts that bounced around them, and then he glanced back at her. "You think I look good? Like this?" Theo pointed to his stubbed leg.

"I do!" Maera answered honestly, and she got to her feet, dusting off her bottom.

"What do we do now?"

"Now?" Maera blinked, not understanding the question.

"Yeah. Now that I know this is a nightmare, I know I'm still in surgery at the hospital. I can't wake myself up because they put me under *ann-eh-stee-zia*... anesthesia. Or whatever they call it."

Her face scrunched up. "What's that?"

"It's a funny kind of medicine you breathe in from a mask that makes you sleep," Theo explained.

"Oh. And you can't wake up?"

"Not until they let me," he answered. "Hey, how old are you anyway?"

"I... I don't really know. I've been here for a very long time, but I can't remember how long it's been. Time works differently in Nightmare. Why? How old are you?"

"I'm eight. I'll be nine in February, though."

"Is that old?" Maera puzzled over the concept of age.

"No. I'm just a kid still. Old is like twenty or thirty. My mom is thirty-two, and my dad is thirty-five. They're pretty old. How old is your dad? The king?"

"He's never told me." She shrugged. "All I know is that he's been here forever, so I'm sure he's ancient." Just then, a loud screech split through the sleeping sky.

"What was that?" Theo asked.

She scowled, feeling troubled. "Colossal."

"The dragon that tried to roast me?"

"Yep, and he's coming this way," Maera grumbled. "We should probably run before he sees us."

"Yeah, probably." Theo wobbled onto his remaining foot before he caught his balance, and then he floated into the air, sticking close by. He eyed the skies warily. "Where can we go?"

"Follow me!" Maera gestured and headed toward Ghost Town, knowing it wasn't far. Racing through the streets, Maera made her way to the old brick building called Restaurant.

"In here!" She hurried inside, holding the door open so Theo could fly through, and then she quickly shut and locked it. Inside, a bunch of booths and tables lined the walls and the center of the room; large windows faced the town's main street. The tables had various plates of food on them for unseen patrons. Another screech caused Maera to look through the nearest window, searching for Colossal.

"What smells so good?" Theo asked.

Maera swiveled around to see Theo walking toward a table. "Don't eat the food!"

It was too late. Theo had already picked up a big, juicy burger.

"No! Put him down!" she warned.

The burger's eyes popped open; he grinned a toothy grin and opened his big mouth to bite Theo's nose.

"Ahhh!" Theo screamed, dropping the burger as he tried chomping at Theo's fingers. Startled, Theo fumbled and fell onto the floor.

Maera rolled with laughter.

"What's so funny?" Theo snapped, his cheeks turning pink with embarrassment.

"Oh, my goodness! Your face! You should have seen your face!" Maera bent over, holding her stomach while she giggled.

"Well, I didn't know," Theo frowned as he tried to stand. He eyed the other plates of food. "Are all of them scary?"

"Go pick one up and see," Maera snickered.

"No, nuh-uh. Nope." Sadly, the moment Theo sat at one of the other tables, a hot dog woke up and split open, showing a long mouth running down the middle of the bun lined with rows of sharp teeth. It nipped the air, trying to bite Theo.

"Ugh! Stop!" He pushed the plate further away. Then, the fries wiggled until they fell over, revealing a top half that looked like fries and a bottom half that looked like wriggling fingers! "Ewww!" He brushed each finger fry away.

"They sure do like you," Maera laughed as they crawled toward him like little caterpillars. "Hardly anyone comes in here anymore. Wait until you see Spaghetti and Soda!" Maera tapped on the plate of spaghetti until it woke up. The plate of spaghetti had many eyes that blinked at them.

"Ahhh!" Theo scooted backward until he sat too close to the blinking noodles.

"Here's Soda." Maera sat and slid a bottle of soda to Theo. Instead of bubbles, Theo saw floating teeth clink against the glass bottle. "I think they're all cute," Maera grinned, watching his fear turn into morbid curiosity.

"You are *so* weird," Theo said, fighting a grin and losing. Maera was happy that Theo seemed less frightened.

"Do you think Colossal is gone?" Theo questioned as he peered at Spaghetti.

"Hmmmm, maybe." Maera rose and looked out one of the windows. She saw Colossal in the distance, soaring back to the castle. "The coast is clear!"

"Then let's get out of here," Theo said, easing out of the booth and being careful that his hands didn't stray too close to the hungrier dishes. He levitated into the air, and together, they left Restaurant. "Where can we go?"

"Well, by now, my father will have many of the Wonders in Nightmare looking for me. I ditched Alessandra, the vampire who was watching me."

"The scary one with the red eyes?" Theo asked, and she nodded. "Except you can fly now. Can't we just fly somewhere else?"

Maera frowned. "I can fly, sure, but not very well. After you left, I died."

"You died?" Theo asked loudly.

"Shhh! You'll attract attention," Maera scolded him in a whisper.

"Sorry," he murmured as he floated closer. "You *died?*" he asked again, but quieter this time.

"Yes, but it's not a big deal, remember? And it sure beat trying to go home the long way," Maera shrugged as she walked. When they spotted a few ghosts, she hurried into an alley and brought her finger to her mouth, signaling Theo to be quiet. They waited until the ghosts passed.

"Maybe we should fly somewhere that they can't find you," Theo suggested in a hushed tone.

"There's only one place they can't go, and it's somewhere that I'm not supposed to go either," Maera replied.

"That's perfect! Where is it?"

"Dream."

"Dream?" Theo looked confused.

"Yes, where the good dreams are. Remember?" Maera reminded him.

"What? We could've gone there this whole time?"

"No! That's what I'm saying. I can't," Maera said grumpily.

"What happens if you do?" Theo asked.

"I'm not sure because no one's ever really told me. Maybe I die?"

"Then you'll be back in the castle in your room, which would suck. What if you didn't, though?"

Maera thought for a moment and then shrugged. "I was always told that those in Nightmare stay in Nightmare, and those in Dream stay in Dream. They never cross over, Theo."

"Just because they don't, doesn't mean they can't," he argued. "Can't we just go see it? Please? Maybe it's not so bad. Maybe you'll be fine."

"It sounds risky," Maera frowned, toeing the ground.

Suddenly, a loud screech caused her head to snap up, and she figured that Colossal was circling back. He was still looking for her.

"We should go! Before he sees us," Theo urged. "Worst case, you end up in your room. What's the harm?"

"All right!" Maera huffed, and she walked out of the alley. She ran down the main dirt road that split the town, trying to sprout her wings as she went. It took a lot of effort, but eventually, her wings sprung out, and she flapped her silvery wings until she felt they were ready to carry her. She leaped into the air, gliding for a short distance before she was back on the ground again. She ran faster and jumped once more, getting higher this time, and her wings flapped even harder until she landed several yards away. "Ugh! Come on!" she growled in frustration.

"Remember, light as a feather," Theo encouraged from ahead. "Feel the wind in your wings and let the air lift you. *Believe* that you *can* do it."

Gritting her teeth, she took a deep breath, willing herself to levitate, believing that she could. With a *woosh*, Maera flew, though she had to concentrate on doing it. But she was still flying. She smiled triumphantly.

"Great job! Where to?" Theo asked when she caught up to him.

"This way," Maera said. She banked to the right, heading toward the Mountains of Terror. "It's past those peaks." She pointed, and Theo whizzed ahead.

"Hey, wait!" she shouted. "It's dangerous!" She hurried to catch up. When she finally did, Theo was close to the mountains, and smaller dragons launched into the air to chase him.

"Maera!" Theo cried out when one tried to attach itself to him. A few others swarmed Theo from below.

"They feed on fear, so don't be afraid, and they'll leave you alone," Maera told him.

"Ouch! It bit me!" Theo yelped as he dropped out of the air. "Maera!"

Maera dove after him.

"Cranky! Scrooge! Buster! Stop! He's my friend!" The small dragons glanced up at her and then back at Theo. One licked its chops, ready to nip him again. "I mean it," Maera warned. With pitiful, sad eyes, the baby dragons flew away, returning to the cave on top of the craggy mountain and leaving Theo alone. Moments later, Theo flew toward her.

"Thanks," he said. He wiped at a few scuffs, but he had no lasting damage. "Whoa, look!" He pointed to where the sky brightened. Fluffy pink and orange clouds danced on the horizon. Purple clouds loomed overhead, and Theo zipped right up to one, bursting through it. "Hey! It tastes...," he licked his lips and frowned, "like... rotten candy! Yuck!" He spat it out while Maera laughed.

Theo suddenly looked at Maera with wide eyes. "Maera! Your wings!"

It was too late. Maera had lost her concentration and was falling fast.

"Maera!" Theo shot after her as she tumbled through the air.

No matter how hard she tried, she couldn't get her wings back. She needed more practice. Theo hurried after her, trying to catch and carry her, but she was too heavy for him, and they both dropped, though not nearly as fast as before.

"Maera! What do we do?" Theo asked, panicking.

"I wish I knew! I can't concentrate enough to get my wings to work!" Maera answered. "Just leave me. Keep heading in that direction, and you'll reach Dream."

"I don't want you to die!" Theo fretted.

"It's okay. I'll just wake up in my room," she told him. "I'll be in trouble, but I'll be fine."

Theo wouldn't leave her. Instead, he tried harder to carry her, pushing himself to fly better. Though he did his best, they still dropped through a couple of fluffy pink clouds as they fell through the air. The snowy mountains rapidly got closer as they plunged from the sky.

Maera closed her eyes, anticipating the sudden yank back to her room in the castle. She waited for the moment Theo's arms would disappear. Strangely, the wind slowed, and they gently fell into soft snow, the impact causing them to untangle and roll apart.

Wait... snow? Maera opened her eyes. She smiled. "I'm not dead!"

"You're still here!" Theo exclaimed at the same time.

"Theo, that was dangerous. I'm not sure what happens if you die in a dream you can't wake from," Maera said.

Theo was covered in snow and frowned before he licked some of it off his chin. "Mmmm!" Theo's frown instantly turned into a grin. "It tastes like *frosting*!" Theo scooped up snow and shoveled it into his mouth. "Try it!"

"Ewww. It's so *sweet*," Maera's face scrunched up, and she spat it out.

"Why are you spitting it out?" Theo asked. "It's good."

"No, it's not. I'd like it better if it were sour milk-flavored or tasted like rotten egg whites. Oh, with sprinkles of crisped ants on top!"

"Gross!" Theo frowned.

"What?" Maera shrugged. "I think that sounds perfectly horrible."

"And that's a *good* thing?" Theo asked in disbelief.

"Yes! Only the scariest of Wonders eat such *horrible* food, and I want to be the *scariest* of them all!"

"You seriously are so weird," Theo shook his head, smiling.

"You have pink fluff in your hair," Maera pointed.

Theo patted his blond hair, feeling for the bits of cloud. He plucked out the fluffy pink wisps, plopped them into his mouth, and laughed. "Yum! These ones actually taste *good*–like cotton candy!" He got up on one foot and held his arms out to find his balance just as it started to snow. "Hey! It's snowing!" He stuck out his tongue to catch some of the snowflakes. A few landed on his outstretched tongue and melted. "Cool! It's sugar!" he laughed. "This place is *awesome*!"

Maera stuck out her tongue and tasted a few snowflakes. "Ick! It's... sweeter than the snow!"

Theo snickered. "Most kids like sweet things."

"Not me!" Maera waded through the deep, frosting-like snow, trekking forward and passing bits of large rock jutting from the snow. When the ground was smoother and the snow was no longer waist-deep, she glanced up and gasped at the view. *I should have known! If sweet snow wasn't a big enough hint!* "Uh oh...." She shouldn't *be* here!

"What? What is it? Is it another scary monster?" Theo's brows pinched together as he hobbled to catch up.

"No," Maera answered, staring into the landscape.

The world was filled with bright colors. To the left, the mountains were tipped in pearly-white frosting, and then the snow gave way to lush green grasses and forests filled with healthy trees, bushy with leaves. The ocean in the distance looked warm and inviting. From their vantage, they could see a huge, brightly colored world.

"It's no monster," Maera frowned while Theo limped over to where she stood. *This is bad. Really bad.* Her heart hammered upon seeing dazzling valleys with sparkling rivers of the brightest blues, reflecting the bright sunlight like bits of silver that glimmered like glitter. Strange lakes of various blues scattered across the expanse. Some were soft turquoise and clear, butting up against the mountains, and others were a deep blue surrounded by trees.

"Oh no," her face fell. "No, no, no!"

"What?" Theo demanded, not understanding what had her so upset.

She gestured sharply. "Just *look*!"

Theo glanced at the unfamiliar mountains, which shimmered with rocks of gold, soft browns, and grays. Pockets of trees were sprinkled around rolling hills of golden wheat in places.

Maera stared at the distant fields filled with rows of different colored tulips. More fields stretched into a sea of big, yellow sunflowers. Meanwhile, cities gleamed in the distance with glassy skyscrapers, and in other parts of the horizon, quaint villages dotted the edges. There was nothing wonderfully ugly here. She was no longer in Nightmare.

"This is bad," she despaired, feeling out of place in this brightly colored world.

"Why? I don't get it. If it isn't a monster, then what? What's wrong?" Theo asked, sounding alarmed.

"Don't you see? This is so much *worse* than a monster," she uttered, covering her face with her hands and shaking her head.

"What's worse than a monster?"

"We... we're... in *Dream!*" Maera cried dramatically.

Theo took that moment to finally appreciate the surroundings.

"No wonder everything here is sweet! And pretty! And *pleasant!*" she exclaimed gloomily, hating the way those awful words tasted in her mouth. She slapped her tongue at the roof of her mouth; the words felt foreign.

"Except you're still here!" Theo happily pointed out with a bright smile. The truth that they were both okay lifted his shoulders. "You didn't die or disappear! This isn't *bad*! This is *great!*"

Theo was so joyful that Maera couldn't help but smile at him... until he bent down, gathered some snow, and threw a ball that splattered across her forehead.

"Hey!" she shouted when he giggled. She grimaced, wiping the sweet muck off her face.

Theo laughed until she returned fire, chucking a snowball at him that exploded across his chest. The look of shock that flashed in his eyes had her grinning from ear to ear before she reached for more snow. Theo leaped into the air, trying to dodge her flying white missile. She threw another, running after him and hitting him in the leg. He swooped down, gathered a handful, and then launched it at her. She ducked, and it sailed harmlessly overhead. Their epic snowball fight had Theo zooming and Maera racing past peaks and crevasses filled with more snow, sending snowballs soaring through the air at one another. Though the snow was much too sweet, Maera couldn't deny that she was having fun. The battle continued as they made their way down the mountain.

"Come on!" Theo finally hollered when the snow thinned, revealing bright green grass shoots beneath. He zipped the rest of the way down the mountain, and Maera ran to keep up. When they reached the bottom, lush grassy hills and beautiful leafy green trees reached toward the bright, sunny blue sky. Flowers of different shapes and sizes speckled the meadows and hills. There were blue ones, pink ones, orange ones, and purple ones. Theo picked a pink flower and handed it to her.

"It's... so ugly," Maera grimaced. "Why is it such a soft color? And where are all the thorns?"

Theo frowned. "These aren't ugly. They're pretty, and I like that they don't have thorns."

Maera popped it in her mouth, hoping that despite its ugliness, it would be useful like the ones in Nightmare. "Ugh! It tastes like... like...." The strange flavor was somewhat familiar, like she had tasted it long ago when she was very young and had completely forgotten about it.

"*Strawberry*!" Theo grinned, chomping on a pink flower.

"Strawberry," Maera said slowly. She felt like she'd tried strawberry once, only she couldn't remember when that could've been.

"Oh! And blueberry!" he said as he ate a blue one. He grabbed an orange one. "Mmmm! Mango!"

Maera tried another flower, purple this time, but again, it was gross and overly sweet. "Grape!" Theo grinned when he tried a purple flower.

Maera swallowed the flower, and then she started running, but to her dismay, she was still slow. "They taste terrible, *and* they don't make me run any faster," she complained. "These are useless."

"Mmmm! This bright red one is cherry! Who cares if they don't make you fast? They taste amazing!" Theo was too busy eating flowers to pay her too much attention. "Oh! Try the grass! It tastes like a green apple!" He held out a handful, and Maera took a blade of grass, reluctant to eat it. "Just try it!" Theo urged, so Maera tasted it.

"It's sour," Maera noted, and then she smiled. "It's sour!" She picked some more grass and ate a few more blades. She *liked* the green apple.

"Holy smokes! The tree bark tastes like chocolate! And the leaves are minty!" Theo was overjoyed. "This place is awesome! And look how cute and pretty the bugs are!" He pointed at the colorful crystal dragonflies and golden bumble bees that floated by. The bees made happy little loops, bouncing from flower to flower, causing Maera's brows to draw together in a slight frown. The crystal dragonflies tinkled a pleasant sound, like musical glass chimes. It was a pretty sound.

Maera rolled her eyes. "Why does everything have to be so *bright* and *cheery*, though?"

"Because! This must be where all the good dreams happen," Theo replied with a huge grin.

I hate it. It's too strange. She frowned. *Is this how other kids feel when they go to Nightmare?* "And... you don't feel scared being here?" she asked quietly, feeling very out of place.

"No way!" Theo laughed. "Why would I?"

Because I do, she thought, but she did not admit it aloud.

Just then, a strange thundering sound rumbled around them.

Maera spun around to see a herd of wild horses galloping by. Each one was a different color of the rainbow. There were baby blue ones with silky dark blue manes and tails, and others were soft pink with deeper pink manes and tails. There were also yellow, orange, and even green horses.

"Whoa! Look at those horses!" Theo exclaimed. "It's like a rainbow herd!"

"There aren't any black ones?" Maera asked with a frown. "And why can't I see any of their bones?"

Theo turned back toward her. "It's okay, Maera. They're just different, is all. You really don't like them?"

"I miss the ones back home," Maera confessed sadly. "I've never left Nightmare before." Theo zipped over to where she stood, scowling at the colorful wild horses. Together, they watched the rainbow herd leap, buck, and prance, playing with one another as they ran by. They were livelier than horses in Nightmare, and their whinnies were pleasant sounding instead of shrieking like she was used to.

"Don't worry. It's okay," he said softly. "Sometimes, when I go to new places, I get scared or homesick too."

"I'm not scared!" Maera scoffed, feeling offended. "I never get *scared*. I'm from Nightmare, remember?"

"But you're homesick," Theo pointed out.

"What's... homesick?"

"It's when you miss your home badly," he answered. "But look at this place! Look at all the cool things that are here! Aren't you at least a *little* curious about what you might find in this place? After all, you said you'd never left Nightmare before."

Maera gazed at her surroundings. In Dream, the sky was a bright blue with fluffy white and vanilla-colored clouds, and the sun shined so brightly that it made everything look much too brilliant. However, Theo had a point. She was a little curious about the place that was so very different from where she lived.

"I guess…," she hesitated, reluctant to admit the truth. "I guess I'm a *little* curious."

Theo grinned wide. "Awesome! Let's see what else we can find here!"

He lifted himself into the air. Maera tried to follow him, but she couldn't seem to summon her wings in Dream and was stuck with walking. She ignored the sweet flowers, crystal dragonflies, and the bumbling golden bees. Maera missed her home and all the familiar Wonders. She felt utterly out of place in her midnight-blue dress. Theo looked like he fit right in. Even his white hospital gown with the little blue dot print seemed brighter here.

CHAPTER

SEVEN

As they explored Dream, the landscape changed, and everything turned spotted with large black and white splotches. A small town ahead looked very strange, with cars that moved slowly around, making low *mooing* sounds. Theo started shaking with laughter.

"What's so funny?" Maera asked.

"It's a cow town! What an odd sort of dream!" he said between peels, holding his belly with one hand and pointing with the other. "Look! Everything looks like a cow! Even the cars! Holy cow! And the houses! Look at the houses! I have to see this up close!" He shot ahead. Maera ran after him, but he was faster. When she caught up, Theo grinned at people passing by in cow print clothes and walking small cows on leashes. The streetlights were all cow-patterned, and even the houses looked like large cows!

"This place is *strange*," Maera said, but she didn't entirely hate it.

"But it's so funny!" Theo chuckled when a cat that looked like a cow ran by and raced up a black and white tree, giving a tiny "*Meoooo.*" Theo zipped by, looking in one of the windows of a cow house. "There are cow couches! And even cow lamps! Maera! Come look." Maera approached a window, gazing at the cow stuff inside.

"Whoa. That's so... *odd!*" She'd never seen anything like it.

Theo chuckled. "Come on!" He took her hand and soared away, dragging her after him. At the edge of Cow Town, they came to a forest. The trees were tall and filled with emerald needles, reminding Maera of something long forgotten.

"What do you think lives in *there*?" he asked.

"Hmmm, I'm not sure, but I hope there are big hungry wolves, angry badgers, or even shadow monsters inside," Maera replied with excitement.

Theo's face turned contemplative. "Maybe there will be nicer creatures instead."

"What's so fun about that?" Maera retorted.

Theo drifted closer and paused, taking in a big breath and closing his eyes. "Mmmm, it smells like pine! It reminds me of Christmas!" As soon as he said it, some of the trees lit up with little lights wrapped around them. Theo's eyes danced with joy. "It *looks* like Christmas! Only, there's no snow. Let's check it out!" Theo flew on ahead, and Maera followed.

Christmas... That word made Maera feel warm inside—excited even. *Strange,* she thought.

She followed Theo through the smears of sunlight that filtered through the trees. The forest felt so inviting; the sunbeams kept the shadows from coming out. The forest floor was carpeted in moss, ferns, or grass. Warm patches of dirt peaked through, making the path so soft that little to no sound was made while they walked. There were no eerie sounds here. Instead, happy croaks from little frogs harmonized with a few crickets and the occasional birdsong.

"Awww! Look!" Theo exclaimed with excitement. Baby deer

and fluffy bunnies scampered by, followed by little furry squirrels. "They're so adorable!"

"I guess," Maera said, but she thought they looked ugly and overly soft. "Where are their bones?"

"On the inside, of course!" Theo laughed.

"What's the point of that?"

"It makes them cuter and cuddlier. Here!" He held out his hand toward a little butterscotch rabbit with a white tail. "Come here," he beckoned softly. "Come on," he urged the baby bunny to come closer. The bunny, looking curious, hopped up to him. "Hello, little fella." Theo picked it up and then floated to Maera. "Here, hold out your arms."

Maera held out her arms, and Theo passed her the bunny.

"It's... *soft*," she noted, the fur different from those in Nightmare.

"Right?" Theo beamed. "Doesn't it feel nice against your skin? You can pet it. It's friendly."

Maera hesitated but then petted it. It was *very* soft, not at all coarse or spiky.

"Well?" Theo asked eagerly.

"It's too soft," Maera said. "And way too friendly." Maera handed the little rabbit back to Theo, who lightly brushed his hand over its fur several times before gently setting it down. He smiled when it bounced back toward its friends.

Theo and Maera ventured deeper into the forest, where every other tree had small, colorful lights draped around them. More baby animals skittered around, seemingly playing together while they raced between shafts of sunlight.

Eventually, the trees thinned as they reached the ledge of a large canyon. When they looked into the canyon, Maera saw the bluest river she had ever seen, cutting through the middle. It was so stunning and sparkly under the sun; it looked like a bejeweled snake. Occasionally, small, beautiful waterfalls ran over the edges of the dark-brown rocky canyon rim; the spray from the water caught the sunlight and reflected brilliant rainbows.

"Wow," Theo gasped. Along the base of the canyon, a collection of trees flanked the picturesque river; the sunrise-colored canopies contrasted against the bright blue river. The white-barked trees occasionally thinned, revealing a hill to pop through in a carpet of soft grass.

"Hey! Those are birch trees! And Aspen!" Theo smiled. "That's how they look in the fall. Aren't they pretty?"

"Sure," Maera replied, feeling overwhelmed by the many bright colors.

"Well, *I* think it's pretty. Look at all the colors! Like those bushes!"

Theo pointed at some bushes between the trees that dotted some of the hills. "Do you see them?" Theo asked. "With brilliant pinkish-red leaves? And look at those vines! Aren't they nice?"

Maera followed his line of sight, spotting vines with fiery leaves clinging to some trees along the dark, rocky outcrops. It was like a paradise of fall colors and much too pretty for Maera's taste. "They are... something."

"Let's go get a better look!" Theo led the way while Maera climbed down the rocky path, zigzagging to the bottom. "Maera!" Theo cried out.

"What? What is it?" Maera hurried to see what was wrong, but Theo hung suspended in the air with a look of wonder on his face.

"*Unicorns!*" he pointed. Healthy white horses with golden horns raced along the shallow banks of the river, splashing and playing. Small pink and yellow orbs that were too big to be fireflies hovered around the white horses, making them look even more magical. "Aren't they neat?" Theo murmured in awe.

"I guess," Maera replied. "They're... fatter than the ones in my realm."

Theo snorted, shaking his head. "The ones in your world look like skeletons. These look more alive! And healthy," he smiled. "Do you think I could pet one?"

"Maybe," Maera shrugged. "I don't know anything about Dream, but if this were Nightmare, they'd try to bite or stab you with their horns if they sensed you were nervous or frightened. Perhaps you could try." Maera was interested to know what they'd do.

"Nah, I won't bother them," Theo replied, not looking quite so certain. "I mean, they look too happy playing in the river, and I wouldn't want to bother them."

"You sure you're not scared?" Maera teased.

"Nope!" Theo said a little loudly, but Maera didn't believe him.

"Hey, what are those lights?" Maera pointed at bobbing lights that seemed to weave between the trees, flitting through the autumn leaves and bobbing through the air. More of them surrounded the playful unicorns.

"They seem to like the unicorns," Maera noted. She noticed small, winged bodies inside the lights that produced a humming sound as they flew, each note unique. Together, it all sounded like a sort of melody.

"Fairies!" Theo hollered. "Wow! Actual fairies." He held out his hand, and one drifted over. He laughed when the fairy began dancing and twirling on his palm before lifting off and flitting away, leaving a twinkling trail of dust behind.

"We have those in Nightmare," Maera volunteered.

"What are they like there?" Theo asked as he flitted through the air to chase a couple.

"The ones there are either really dark blue or purple and have stingers on their hands. If you try to catch one, they either bite or sting you."

Theo frowned. "They don't sound so nice."

"They're perfectly terrible," Maera remarked proudly. Smiling, she forged on, leaving Theo to fly after her.

They weaved between the trees with colorful fall leaves at the bottom of the canyon while the sun cast a warm glow as if it were early morning. The grass in the wooded area was speckled with fallen leaves, making it look just as colorful as the trees. Different kinds of birds chirped and sang, blending in with the melodious hum of fairy wings.

"I can't believe you've never come to Dream," Theo said as he floated beside her.

"Nightmares have no place here," Maera replied as if it were obvious.

"Except... you don't even look like a nightmare. Far from it, actually." Theo frowned. "And you're nicer than anyone I've seen in Nightmare."

Maera spun to face him. "Take that back!"

"What?" Theo asked in surprise. "That's a good thing! Why would I take it back?"

"Take it back!"

"But... it's true. You don't look like anything in Nightmare," Theo argued.

Maera stared at Theo, feeling hurt and angry. "All I ever wanted was to be the scariest Wonder in Nightmare," she bitterly confessed. "I can't believe you would say that to me."

"I'm sorry," Theo said. He did not mean to offend her, but the words still stung. "If that's what you want to do, then why aren't you scaring people?"

"Because! I haven't found my purpose yet!" She hated that it made her feel less valuable than all the other Wonders in Nightmare.

"How do you do that?" Theo drew closer. "Find your purpose, I mean?"

"I...." Maera deflated, all the anger leaving her so swiftly that her shoulders drooped. "I don't know." She thought for a moment, and then her head snapped up. "Though I don't think I'll find it *here*. I don't belong in Dream. This isn't my home." Maera ran. "I want to go home."

"Hey! Wait! Maera!" Theo flew after her, but she didn't stop.

Maera ran as fast as she could until she reached the edge of the trees, where a huge cliff with a river ran over the edge, creating mist as the water cascaded over it.

"Whoa," Theo murmured while he hung in the air above the river as it dumped into a small pool before flowing into a valley beyond. Massive pieces of land seemed to have broken away, lifting from the sides of the canyon and hovering like suspended islands in the air. Each floating island was lush with mini rain-forests.

"I've never seen floating islands before. Look! Some of those are pretty high up there," Theo pointed. "And look at the trees growing on some of them. Have you seen so many flowers?"

The trees were adorned with peach or white flowers and were home to cute black and white monkeys and colorful birds that chirped and whistled in exotic birdsong.

"Just look at all those birds," Theo watched in awe. "How many kinds can you spot?"

Maera squinted, peering through the mist that enveloped the islands. "Hmm. That island, the closest one... I can see some strange ones with blue and turquoise wings," Maera calmly noted.

"And those ones over there have different feathers. You see? The ones with huge wings and the long plumes for tails?" Theo pointed out.

Maera watched the birds of different sizes glide and flit from one suspended island to another, declaring, "There are even some that look like cardinals, and those look like toucans with their funny beaks. Oh, are those parakeets?"

"I think so," Theo nodded "Hey, you're pretty good at knowing the different birds."

She grinned. "Um, thanks! There are just so many!"

"Look over there! The monkeys! They're playing chase!" Theo laughed as he watched the monkeys swing from branches to vines, occasionally flying through the air before catching another vine or branch and scurrying higher into the trees. "How high up do you think those islands go?"

Maera shrugged. "I can't really see much beyond the closer ones, and with the sun behind the clouds, the mist looks really thick," Maera declared. The mist from multiple waterfalls surrounded the floating islands, and the nearby huge waterfall churned more spray into the air where she stood.

Theo smiled. "Hey, the sun is coming back out from behind that cloud." The world burst into rainbows, connecting islands with bridges of reflective color.

"So. Many. Rainbows," she said with a disturbed shudder. It was so dazzling that it made her *sick*!

"With the sun shining, you can see we're really high," Theo noted. "I think we should turn around and see if there's a safer way down."

Maera wasn't sure how long that would take, and she was eager to return to Nightmare and the comforts of home. She glanced around, trying to figure out what to do.

Beyond the rocky ledge and the hovering islands, the canyon walls shrank, opening to reveal a breathtaking valley beyond. In the center, an impressive castle of white crystal shimmered like a beacon. Unexpectedly, a gust of wind encircled her, and she was swarmed by giant, colorful butterflies.

Maera had an idea. She backed up, and a wicked grin pulled at her lips.

"Maera, what are you doing?" Theo asked with a note of concern. "We should go back and find another way down."

Suddenly, Maera ran.

"Maera!" he called after her.

Maera leaped off the waterfall's misty ledge, landing on the back of a massive butterfly. Its huge wings were adorned in pockets of yellow and white between black lace. Her butterfly flew alongside another that was purple and pink.

"No way!" Theo shot forward. He then dropped onto the back of a teal and green one. "Woo Hoo!" he shouted. "Maera! This is freaking AWESOME! Best idea ever!" They rode the giant butterflies toward the valley below. "Go butterfly! Go!" Theo urged his butterfly to swoop toward the tranquil lake at the base of the huge waterfall.

"Hey, Maera, look at me!" Theo reached down as his butterfly leveled out, and his fingers grazed the clearest water she'd ever seen. Snickering, he flicked the water, pelting Maera with cool droplets.

"Stop!" Maera shrieked when he moved to do it again. She swiftly dipped her fingers into the water as she skimmed the lake, creating a splash that rippled across the glassy surface. She laughed upon seeing that she managed to spray Theo quite thoroughly.

The friends joyfully glided across the water, playfully splashing water at each other, and at that moment, Maera forgot any thoughts of homesickness. Soon, the butterflies beat their giant wings and rose higher into the air. The canyon opened, and the edges morphed into crystal mountains of coral that sparkled under the sun wherever the rock was exposed.

"How much do you want to bet that the snow on the tops of those mountains also tastes like frosting?" Theo pointed and grinned.

"You're probably right," she grimaced.

"I wonder if it tastes like the other snow frosting or if it is other flavors."

"I don't know why you like frosting so much," she pulled a face. "Doesn't the sickly sweetness make your stomach ache?"

"Yes, in the best way! And it's worth it!" He flashed her a crooked grin, and she couldn't help but giggle a little.

"And you say *I'm* weird," she shook her head. Below the snow-line, the dramatic ridges gave way to forests. The rolling hills and beautiful scenic landscapes stretched out before them. They followed the river as it snaked through the valley like a jeweled necklace that caught the sunlight.

"Look! A city!" Theo pointed. "And a castle!"

"I see it. It's... a *strange*-looking castle," she commented. It wasn't like the dark, gothic one she lived in. Dream's castle had multiple towers that looked inviting rather than imposing. Its spired roofs looked like they were dipped in gold ink. The city surrounding the castle was made of the same elegant white rock, gently tapering down the hill it was all built upon.

"All those fields on the city's outskirts are different colors," Theo brightened. "I've never seen fields that looked so nice."

"I think they're flowers," Maera said.

Getting a little closer, it became clearer. The outside of the city was a patchwork of colorful fields. Some were filled with bright poppies and irises. Others were filled with lavender, larkspur, or tulips. The scenery looked like a perfectly picturesque painting. The sweet floral scents from the various flowers drifted on the wind, causing Maera's homesickness to return. Dream was over-whelmingly different from Nightmare. Her heart squeezed at the thought.

The butterflies brought her and Theo closer to the castle. That wasn't where Maera wanted to go, but she was stuck. She couldn't get her wings to work, so she had to wait until the large butterflies got close enough to the ground that she could ditch it and jump off.

When they fluttered low enough to the grass, Maera happily

slid off, rolling to slow her momentum in a somewhat graceful manner.

"Maera!" Theo cried out with alarm before she popped back up.

"I'm fine!" She grinned, straightening her dress and brushing herself off. "See?"

Theo's worry turned into relief, and he dismounted his butterfly by floating closer to Maera. They watched as the large creatures soared away.

"Now what?" Theo looked around.

"I haven't figured that out yet. I'm not sure how to get out of here." Maera frowned, taking in their new surroundings. "This place is huge. I...," she hesitated, knowing that she was about to disappoint her friend, "I need to find my way back to Nightmare."

Theo's face fell. "You really want to go back? To the Nightmare land?"

As she had predicted, he seemed crestfallen.

"Can't we just stay here for a little longer?" he asked with pleading eyes.

"I need to return," Maera answered slowly. "My father is probably really worried. I've been gone a while now. I wasn't supposed to come here, and I still need to find my purpose."

The sudden sounds of trumpets startled the two of them, and she spun around to see knights approaching in shining gold armor while riding large white horses. "Uh oh," she scowled, feeling anxious as they got closer. She took a step backward, then another. "I think they're here to take me away and lock me up since I'm from Nightmare."

"You think they'll put you in a dungeon?" Theo looked genuinely worried.

"Why else are they charging over here?" Maera asked. "Maybe I should run and hide."

"If they try to lock you up, I'll stop them," Theo said bravely, and Maera smiled.

"You think you can?"

"Of course!" he exclaimed, though he seemed a little doubtful. "But maybe you should run just in case."

She had already considered it. At least a dozen knights were coming toward them. Maera quickly looked for a place to hide, but the mountains and forest were too far.

"I'll distract them. You go and hide!" Theo declared as he veered in a different direction.

Maera ran with everything she had, but there were few places to hide in the rolling grassy hills. She turned to look back, and the knights blew past Theo and came after her. Maera tried to hurry, urging her wings to sprout. Before she could get too far, and before she could get her wings to work, a knight reached down and scooped her up.

"No! Put me down!" She kicked and fought, but it was no use. The knight was too strong, and he was protected by his armor, holding her firmly in place.

"Maera! I'm coming!" Theo hollered.

The knights circled back, and one sprang forward, plucking Theo right out of the air.

"Hey!" Theo protested, thrashing like Maera. They both struggled until they were tired. Neither was getting free anytime soon. Maera accepted her fate with a glare.

The captors rode past the various flower fields, through the little city within the castle walls, and up toward the center where the crystal castle waited. It sparkled, looking far too perfect with its flawless, multi-level symmetrical spires, keeps, and towers. Maera hated it and missed her sleek obsidian castle home in Nightmare.

Once they reached the castle, they were greeted by people in fancy gowns and suits who cheered and threw flower petals at them as they passed by. It was as if they were happy with their arrival. The horses carried them to the castle's front doors, where the knights dismounted. Maera's knight picked her up and carried her inside, preventing her from running away. Another picked up Theo.

The inside of the castle was worse than the outside! The walls were adorned with golden flowers and vines. Large paintings of sunsets, horses, and other happy pictures lined the halls and walls of the rooms. Rows of guards in shiny armor stood at attention.

The knights marched through the castle until they reached the throne room. A long pale blue carpet led to the grand throne. Like her father's throne room, a balcony loomed overhead where a huge hourglass was filled with trickling golden sand instead of red like the one in her home. Maera's eyes dropped from the hourglass and settled upon the Queen of Dreams. Her bright, blonde hair, smooth porcelain skin with rosy cheeks, and stunning eyes were difficult to find ugly; it was like looking into a translucent glacier. She had a pleasant smile, but Maera didn't trust it at all. The queen held a pale wooden staff with a gold orb at the top. She wore a gilded crown on her head, just like the stained-glass portrait in the Castle of Nightmare.

"Welcome," the queen said in a voice that sounded like a song. It was too beautiful–*she* was too beautiful. "Welcome, welcome. Maera, it's been such a long time, but I'm so very glad to see you again! When my little birds told me you were back, I couldn't believe my ears!" The majestic queen stood. "Come closer. Let me get a good look at you." Maera's knight urged her to walk forward and meet the queen. In her poofy ballroom gown, the queen was like a pearl that glided toward Maera, her skirts swishing as she moved.

"My, my," she said, looking Maera over with a twinkle in her lavender eyes. She smelled like roses and vanilla. "You've grown some. Tell me, how old are you now? Eight? Nine?"

Maera frowned. "I... don't know."

"Hmmmm. And who's your friend?" the queen inquired.

Theo hobbled over, and the queen brightened. "Ah, right! Theodore! Dear sweet Theo, yes, I remember you. It's been some time since you visited Dream. Although it has not been quite as long as Maera."

"Yeah, I keep getting stuck in Nightmare." Theo grimaced. "That's actually where we came from."

The queen's smile faltered slightly.

"It is?" She looked between the two of them. "Most unusual!"

Just then, a little bluebird fluttered in and chirped into the queen's ear.

"Oh?" the queen replied to the little bird. "You don't say! Really?" The bird fluttered away, and the queen redirected her attention to the children. "Well, I think I understand now. Maera, the King of Nightmares has requested your immediate return. I'm not supposed to interfere in the affairs of Nightmare, so I will have to send you back."

"But," Theo protested, "can't she just stay for a little while longer?"

"No, young Theo. Besides, it is time for *you* to wake up."

Before Theo could argue, the queen gently tapped the end of her staff on Theo's head, and he disappeared.

The queen then turned to Maera. "All right. Although I am delighted that you chose to come to Dream for a visit, it's time to go back. I do hope to see you again soon, though." She smiled pleasantly before tapping Maera's head.

Maera blinked, and suddenly, she was in her father's throne room.

The King of Nightmare sat on his throne, looking concerned.

"Maera, you're back. I was so worried. Tell me, why were you in Dream?"

"Father, I... I was...." She bit her lip.

"The truth this time," her father barked.

She folded her hands and kicked at the ground, hating that she'd upset him and reluctant to confess all she'd done. One swift glance and she knew his patience was thin. *There's no getting around it.* She blew out a breath, reaching for courage. "I wanted to hang out with Theo. Father, he said he couldn't wake up! He said the doctors gave him something... Anastasia, I think."

"Anesthesia," he corrected.

"Yes, that. So he couldn't wake up. Doc took his foot, and then he was stuck here. I knew Alessandra would tell on me, and then you'd send someone to fetch me. I just wanted to hang out with Theo for a while. He already lost his foot, you see, so the nightmare played out this time."

Her father's lips thinned.

She forged on before he could interrupt. "And that's when he suggested that we go somewhere no one would chase us, and then, well, we were flying. Only, I fell, and we landed in Dream. After that, he wanted to see what it was like. I suppose I did, too."

"So, you followed the boy? Why didn't you return? You know that those in Nightmare can't cross into Dream."

"Why was Theo able to?" Maera asked.

"He's a Sleeper. That's a little different."

Maera's eyebrows pinched together. "Okay, then why could I?"

The king frowned. "You don't know?"

Maera shook her head.

The king studied her for a moment. "I suppose it's because you're special." His features softened some. "You are my sweet Night Maera, after all."

"Father?" Maera took a step toward the throne. "Why did the

queen say she was surprised to hear that I'd returned? How come she knew me? I don't remember ever going there or seeing her."

The king's eyes seemed to stare beyond Maera, and he took a long time before answering. "If you don't remember her, then perhaps she was mistaken. If you don't recall going to Dream, then there's no way you could have met her. Tell me, while in Dream, did anything seem... familiar?" He asked her with such seriousness that it made her nervous.

Maera fidgeted with her blue dress. "No," she replied, having already forgotten the taste of the strawberry flowers and warmth she felt in the Christmas Forest. "Nothing seemed familiar." Maera frowned. She recalled how everything was overly pretty and bright in Dream and how much she had missed Nightmare while she was there, wishing the entire time for something familiar. "The only time I remember ever seeing the queen was in the picture within the stained glass, up there." Maera pointed to the balcony where the hourglass was.

The king frowned, stroking his chin in thought. "I see. Then perhaps she was mistaken. Only you would know the answer to that, otherwise."

"She must be! I've been here my whole life... ever since I was born. Oh, Father, I hated it in Dream! Everything was too bright, too colorful, and too sweet!" Maera declared passionately. "Everyone was too nice, and they smelled too good. Also, the Wonders there were soft and fluffy! It was awful."

The king laughed. "Yes, that is Dream, all right."

"I just wanted to come back home and find my purpose."

"Nothing there... sparked anything?" the king pressed skeptically.

She frowned, and then she vaguely remembered. *There was that moment near the pine forest... and again when I'd tasted the flowers.* Maybe that was all in her mind. After all, she'd only ever lived in Nightmare, so none of that made any sense. "No," she lied. "Nothing sparked anything, and I thought I had to be here to find my purpose. Don't I?"

"Perhaps." He drummed his fingers on the carved wood of his throne with a thoughtful expression. "But it's getting late." He slowly stood. "You should go and get ready for bed."

"Father?" Maera looked up at him, puzzled.

"Yes?"

"Why can't *we* have nightmares or dreams?"

"Because those who live here in the Land of Dreams don't need them. Nightmares and dreams are meant to carry Sleepers to our realm, bringing them here so they can escape the Waking World. In the Land of Dreams, magic is real, and anything is possible. Our world inspires Sleepers to invent things, to create and explore. It also helps them come to terms with their problems or challenges and helps them in the Waking World. But in our realm, we live simpler lives, so it's not necessary for us to have dreams or nightmares. We *are* the dreams. We *are* the nightmares. It wouldn't make sense for us to dream of ourselves now, would it?"

"Oh. Right. No." It made sense... sort of.

"It's getting late. Run along, little one." The king waved his hand, and Maera trudged back to her room in the tower. She was happy to be back in her horrid castle, but she felt that tug at her heart that left her uncertain. *If only I had a purpose here*, she thought.

CHAPTER

EIGHT

I t had been weeks since Maera returned from Dream, and she hadn't seen or heard anything from Theo. *He must not have come back to Nightmare.* She was sure if he had, she'd have learned of it.

Since her return, she found that she missed her friend. While she longed to see Theo, she stewed on what her purpose might be. No matter how hard she tried, and no matter what she did, she couldn't seem to figure it out.

What if I have no purpose? The idea left her feeling gloomy.

Nearly two whole months passed before Maera finally received word that Theo had returned to Nightmare. Time worked differently here than in the Waking World, so it was hard to say how long it had been for him. Sadly, Maera was under strict rules NOT to go anywhere near Theo. However, there wasn't anyone that could stop her. Her father didn't understand that her intentions had always been to help Theo whenever he was afraid.

That was what nightmares were for, weren't they? To help Sleepers face their fears? At least, that was how she thought it worked.

For weeks, Maera had been tailed by either Bones or Alessandra. Because it had been a long time and Theo hadn't been seen or heard from, Maera had let them do their jobs without complaint. It wasn't until early that morning–when one of Maera's bat friends flew through her bedroom window and chittered at her that Theo was back–that she decided to visit Colossal.

Ditching Bones and Alessandra in a game of "Hide and Go Seek" was easy, and Maera scurried off in search of the dragon. She hoped that she might convince Colossal to fly her around Nightmare so that she could easily see what Theo was up to. He was better at flying, being a dragon and all, and she was less likely to die and be sent back to the castle where Alessandra and Bones would find her.

She headed toward the active volcano, figuring that Colossal was likely lounging near the lava pools. It was hot there, and the ground was black with steaming rocks. Occasionally, deep pockets opened to reveal red, glowing magma that bubbled and spewed bits of hot lava. Colossal loved those, sometimes pouncing on the little pools as if they were puddles, splashing orange, molten rock in all directions.

It didn't take long to find the dragon, and as she suspected, Colossal was happily soaking in the expansive Hellfire Lake, a huge pool of glowing, red lava. She had to ask her question carefully so Colossal wouldn't suspect what she was up to. She marched to the edge of the lake and waved at the bathing dragon.

The gigantic reptile nodded his horned head and swam a little closer to her. His black scales smoked wherever the lava touched him. The dragon savored the heat, and she hoped this would mean he'd be in a better mood.

"Oh Colossal, it's been close to two months, and I still haven't found any clue about what my purpose is." Maera plopped onto a sweltering rock and watched Colossal splash around. He dove under the lava and then resurfaced, his scales steaming. He spat some of the lava out like one would water. A belch of flames followed.

"You don't even care," Maera complained.

Colossal released a slow growl followed by a couple of hisses and the snap of his teeth.

"Okay, maybe you do care," she shrugged.

Colossal then grunted and grumbled.

"No," Maera shook her head. "It's not what you think; it *is* important that I find my purpose. Every Wonder has one except me."

Colossal tilted his head, blinking slowly before he snorted a puff of smoke and made a clicking sound in the back of his throat.

"You don't think I need one," Maera pouted. "Easy for *you* to say. You *have* a purpose."

Colossal didn't reply.

"I was hoping you would cheer me up by taking me on a ride around Nightmare."

Colossal hissed and snapped his teeth.

"You don't feel like it," Maera sulked, feeling disappointed. She watched a few raptors chasing nearby Sleepers. Maera liked the dinosaurs, but only the scary ones could be found in Nightmare. Maera watched them shriek and snap their teeth. The Sleepers were terrified, but even that didn't cheer her up.

Colossal lazily sloshed about the lava lake.

"I can see that you don't seem worried at all about whether or not I'll find my purpose, so I'll leave you to your bath." Maera got up and crossed her arms, waiting to see how Colossal would react. He splashed around in the molten magma some more, unwilling to leave the relaxing hot pool. The lava lakes were his favorite places to hang out, and she should have known he'd be too reluctant to leave them. "Maybe the clowns at the Carnival of Creeps will be better company."

Colossal snorted with a shake of his large head.

"I know," she sighed. "They're not very bright, but at least they'll try to cheer me up, which is more than what *you're* doing,"

Maera flung at her dragon before spinning around and stomping away.

The carnival was about an hour's walk from Hellfire Lake. She picked up her pace, not wanting to walk forever. She tried to sprout her wings, and after a couple of minutes, she was finally able to get them to come out. As she rose into the air, she smiled and flapped her silver feathered wings. Flying was way better than walking, and it was a much faster way of getting around. She'd been practicing flying over the weeks and was getting better with each time. Still, she occasionally fell whenever her mind wandered. If she didn't want Alessandra or Bones to find her, she'd need to be careful not to end up back at the castle by falling to a momentary death.

Maera flew toward the carnival. She passed over the Forest of Screams and Shadows and chuckled when she saw Brigga and Hagetha chasing a few Sleepers. She turned west and zipped past the Haunted Plains, where Sleepers ran from ghosts or zombies, weaving between the many headstones.

A while later, she passed the Hills of Trolls when something caught her eye. Something that looked like it was coming right toward her.

"Wait...," not something, *someone*. "Theo?" Maera hailed, trying to get his attention. He still wore that funny-looking gown. "Theo!" She waved happily, and he immediately changed direction, heading her way. But he didn't smile when he saw her.

"Maera! Hurry! We gotta go!" Theo exclaimed as he blew right past her. It didn't take long before she saw why. A swarm of giant wasps chased him and were closing in; though Maera was thrilled, she had worried she might never see him again.

"Maera, hurry!" he yelled.

"Coming!" She turned around and flapped after him. "Where to?" she asked, hurrying to catch up.

"Dream! Now!"

"Wait, I can't go there!" Maera came to a stop, suspended in the air.

"Yes, you can. Come on! There's something I need to tell you!"

Before she could argue, Theo zoomed toward the craggy, twisted, brown rocks of the Mountains of Terror. Maera's curiosity and desire to be with her friend fueled her pursuit. The swarm of baseball-sized wasps hummed after them. They sped toward the mountains when the wind picked up, causing several large boulders to break away from the mountains and tumble down in a shower of rocks.

"Wait! Slow down!" Maera hollered. She still hadn't mastered flying, and the wasps were now hot on *her* trail, not that they'd bother her. However, the winds quickly became an issue. No matter how close she tried getting to the mountains, the wind blew her back. Theo seemed to have no problem with it at all.

"Theo!" she cried out. A storm was rolling in, and the dark, black clouds were heading their way fast. She flapped her silver wings harder. The wasps couldn't follow them this close to Dream's border, but sadly, she struggled, too. Theo noticed her falling behind and went back for her.

"Take my hand!" he shouted over the gusty wind.

Together, they flew over the mountains and into Dream, but the wind pushed them out close to the ocean. In Dream, it was sunny, making the water look bright turquoise. The wind immediately turned into a gentle, salty breeze with a hint of coconut in the air. No longer struggling against the gale, Maera and Theo floated down to the ground. That's when Maera noticed Theo's leg. It was a little shorter than the last time she saw him.

"Your leg," she pointed. "It changed."

Theo frowned. "Yeah, the doctors took more than I thought they would. So now I'm in recovery. I fell asleep and ended up seeing the scary doctor again; only he was putting all these needles and tubes into me." He hopped along after her as she walked toward the ocean.

"How did you get away?" Maera asked. By this point, Theo gave up on hopping and took to the air, floating after her, which was much faster. When she turned to look, she saw he had a big grin on his face.

"Well?" she asked, dying with curiosity.

"Okay, at first, I wasn't sure I was asleep, but when I saw that doctor *smile*, I realized I was in a nightmare again. I *knew* he looked familiar, and I finally remembered him from last time. Then I recalled what you said about being able to change my dream or, well, in this case, my nightmare. So, I pretended that the tubes were pumping in green liquid, and I suddenly turned green and was *very* strong! Like, really, *really* strong!" he said excitedly. "The green stuff helped me grow my foot back, and then I yanked out all the needles and tubes and ran. The doctor chased me, and here's the coolest part! I ran into a wall, but I went *through* it. I ran through a wall, Maera! It was so cool!"

"I've never seen anyone walk through walls before," Maera confessed.

"You can't walk through walls?"

She shook her head. "No. What happened next?"

"So then, I kept walking through walls until I was outside, but I was too high, and I fell, but it didn't hurt," he assured her quickly. "I tried to fly then, but I was too heavy, so I turned back into me... but my foot was gone again. It was gone, but then I could fly again, so that's when I spread my arms and flew like a plane. Only when I went looking for you did these angry wasps try to stop me."

"Hmmm. But... you actually changed your dream?" she asked, remembering when her father had said few could do that in Nightmare.

"Yeah! You should've seen it! I was smashing through every-thing! The doctor ended up running from *me!*"

"You scared Doc?" Maera couldn't believe it! Sleepers didn't *scare* Wonders.

Theo beamed. "I did! I totally did! I was a bad dude!"

Maera laughed. "Gosh, I wish I could have seen that!"

"Me too," he replied. "Hey. Where are we going?" They reached a golden sandy beach that sparkled under the sun as if it had flecks of actual gold mixed into it. Feeling impulsive, Maera slipped off her slippers and stepped onto the sand. The sand was perfectly warm and not too hot, while the salty air felt like a caress against Maera's cheeks. Though the beach was far too bright, and the colors seemed too vibrant, something about it felt... comforting.

"This looks kind of like the tropics," Theo noted. "My parents said when I got better, they'd take me there one day."

"Tropics?" Maera stopped at the edge of the tideline where the wet sand met gentle waves that sent white foamy water swishing over her toes.

"That's just what my parents call it," Theo replied. "Where I live, the ocean is dark and very cold. The beaches aren't very warm, but we like to go and dig up clams sometimes... or we used to before I got sick."

Maera didn't often hear about the Waking World. "What's it like?" she asked curiously. "The Waking World, I mean."

"Well, I'm in Seattle, in the hospital, and it's not very fun."

"Seattle?" Maera blinked.

"Yeah, the city. It has lots of buildings, some of them are very tall. We live by Point Defiance. It's nice there, but it rains a lot. It isn't as busy as Seattle."

"The zoo," she blurted, not understanding where that came from, yet she had spoken it without even thinking.

"What? The zoo? Yeah, it has a zoo," Theo grinned while he

hovered next to her, drifting closer to the clear blue water. She turned and began walking along the beach, occasionally splashing whenever the water raced across the sand.

"What's a zoo?" Maera asked after a while. "Why do I know that word?"

"You don't have one in Nightmare?"

"I don't think so," Maera replied, searching her memory. "We might... but I... I don't remember seeing one."

"A zoo is where you go to see all kinds of wild animals. They have these *enclosures*... that's what my dad calls them. It's where the animals live, and it's made to look kind of like the wild, so the animals are more comfortable. The one where I live has tigers, wolves, monkeys, and sea turtles—all *kinds* of animals from all around the world. You can go up to their pens and look through the windows and over the fences to see them."

Maera frowned. "They live in a closed-up pen?"

"I suppose they do," Theo replied with a shrug.

"That's... sad." Maera quietly walked on the wet sand, watching the water trickle over her toes with each wave that crashed. "I suppose if I ever had a nightmare, I would think that being trapped in an... what did you call it?"

"Enclosure," Theo replied.

"Right. I would think if I were trapped in an enclosure or a tight spot, unable to move around much, that would be scary. Then, having people standing around looking at me while I was stuck there... and no one coming to help get me out." Maera shivered, letting her voice trail off.

Theo peered over at her. "Can you have nightmares?"

"No. Wonders who live in Dream or Nightmare don't have nightmares or dreams. We're only there to help Sleepers like you have them."

"Oh." Theo frowned for a moment. "But...," he began, then he gasped. "Hey! Look! Is that a *pirate* ship?"

Maera glanced toward the little village ahead, where a large, three-mast pirate-looking ship was anchored in the charming harbor. "I... I think it is." Maera tried to imagine what sort of pirates lived in Dream.

"Come on! Let's go take a closer look!" Theo zipped ahead, and Maera ran after him. They reached the dock and watched men in loose, billowing white shirts with tattoos on their chests and arms hauling crates and barrels onto the ship. Maera couldn't understand why, but something about it seemed oddly familiar.

"Ahoy there!" The tall man with dark dreads of hair, a pirate hat, a peg leg, and a bright green coat waved at them.

Maera swore she'd seen this pirate before, except she remembered him with both legs. *But how could that be? This pirate was from Dream.*

"Are you a pirate?" Theo asked.

The man stood on the plank that connected the ship to the dock. "Aye, young lad. A captain at that, and what be your name?" the pirate asked Theo with a grin. He was missing a couple of teeth and had a couple more capped in gold.

"I'm Theo, and that's Maera."

"Maera," the captain smiled. "Why, you look just like a young lass I saw long ago before I lost me leg."

"Really?" Maera's eyes widened. "Have you ever traveled to Nightmare then?"

"Bah, of course not, lassie!" The captain slapped his leg and laughed. "Those are dangerous waters, those are."

"Oh, that's where I was born," Maera replied.

"Born, you say? Hmmm. Perhaps I be mistaken then." The pirate scratched under his chin and then shrugged.

Theo regarded the large pirate with curiosity. "Who are you?"

"The name be Captain Willabee, but me friends call me Stub."

"Why?" Maera couldn't help but ask.

The captain let out a big belly laugh. "Because, lassie, I have a *stub* for a *leg*!" He wiggled his peg leg that was attached to a small stump of a thigh. "Lost it to the blasted Mad Dragon long ago."

"Mad Dragon?" Theo gulped.

"Aye, but don't worry. No angry sea dragons live here in *these* waters," the captain reassured them. "Say, would you like to sail with me crew? We could use a few more hands on deck."

"Really?" Theo replied excitedly.

"Aye," the captain answered.

"But... my leg." Theo suddenly frowned, and the captain laughed, heartily slapping Theo on the back from where he floated in the air.

"Not a worry, me boy!" Captain Willabee guffawed. "I can fix you right up, and you'll fit right in. What do you say, laddie?"

Theo looked at Maera with hopeful eyes. "Can we?"

Maera sighed. "I suppose."

"Jolly good!" the pirate chuckled. "Follow me!" The captain led the way across the plank and onto the ship. Pirates buzzed about handling rope and rigging, hauling barrels and crates aboard, and taking them below deck.

"This here be me crew," the captain gestured at the various pirates. "They be hard-working men... and women," he corrected, just as Maera noticed a few lady pirates. "Come, I'll show you the captain's quarters." Captain Willabee took them toward the back of the boat. They went through a door nestled between two sets of stairs below the upper deck. Inside was a room with a row of windows at the back and a nice bed off to one side. On the other side was a table covered in maps.

"Over here," the captain beckoned. "Have a seat." Maera and Theo sat down while the captain rummaged through a trunk. "Ah ha! Here we be." He pulled out a wooden peg leg matching his own and a strip of cloth. "Now, this here be a little too big for you, laddie, but I can fix that mighty quick." He went to another trunk, pulled out a saw, and then kneeled in front of Theo. He used the cloth to bind Theo's limb and then fitted the peg leg to it. Using the attached belts, he secured the peg in place.

"Now hold out your legs, me boy, so I know how much of the wood to saw off," the captain instructed. Theo kicked his leg and the peg leg out. The peg was several feet too long. "Okay, now hold still, me boy," the captain ordered, and then he sawed the wood until it was even with Theo's foot. "Now, lad, try standing on it." He helped Theo get to his feet. Theo wobbled a bit but managed to walk around the room a few times.

"There you go, laddie! There you go!" The pirate captain grinned as Theo walked around, testing it out. The peg leg *thumped, thumped* against the wooden flooring while Maera and the captain watched. "Aye! Jolly good, but you be missing something." The older man thought for a moment, then grinned. "I got it!" The captain shuffled over toward his bed and pulled a hat from the trunk at the base.

"Here, this be perfect," Captain Willabee said as he plopped it onto Theo's head. It wasn't as big as the one the captain wore, but Theo looked thrilled to be given it. "And here, lassie." He handed Maera a scarf. "You tie it over your head like this...." The captain draped it over her head, then tied two ends behind her head to hold it in place. "Yep! Now you be looking like part of me crew!"

CHAPTER

NINE

Theo and Maera emerged from the captain's quarters dressed like pirates. Captain Willabee followed them to the deck above. "Gather the ropes and unfurl the sails, lads!" he loudly instructed. "We be going underway!" The crew raced around, getting the ship ready to leave the docks. Several poked long oars out from holes on the sides of the ship below deck, and they were rowed backward. The captain took the helm, and slowly, the crew guided the ship out of the port.

"This is so *cool*!" Theo said excitedly.

"You two scallywags," a thick, burly pirate barked, "go up to the prow and keep an eye out for coral reefs!"

Theo blinked, looking confused. "What's a prow?"

"What's a scallywag?" Maera asked at the same time.

"Why, the prow be the front-most part of the bow of the ship above the water," the pirate replied. "The stern be the back, and a scallywag be a newbie, like you two. Now be gone with you and keep watch for coral heads." Maera and Theo hurried to the very front of the ship and looked down at the water.

"What do you see? There be anything poking out or close to

the surface that the boat might run aground on?" the heavyset pirate asked.

"No!" Maera and Theo shouted. They watched for coral reefs, but thankfully, the ship wasn't headed toward any. The blue water only revealed sand below. When they drifted out past the harbor, the crew pulled in the oars. More sails were dropped and then tightened to catch the wind. They soon sailed out onto the open ocean!

"All right, all right," the burly pirate approached them. "My name be Blight, seeing how I survived smallpox, scarlet fever, and a few other unsavory illnesses." Maera instantly liked his name. "Now, have either of you handled a sword before?" Blight asked in a rumbly voice.

"No," Maera and Theo both said at the same time, shaking their heads.

"Good. You're about to learn," the pirate chuckled. He waved a couple of crew members over with wooden swords. "Now, it's not too hard. All you got to do is strike your opponent. You can stab them or swipe at them with the sides of the sword. Then your opponent has to block your strikes, keeping your sword from hitting them. Got it?" They both nodded. "Good!"

Maera and Theo were handed the wooden swords. Then two crew members paired up with them and taught them how to fight.

"Good! Very good!" Blight smiled as he observed. They went back and forth across the deck of the ship until Maera and Theo were better at striking and blocking hits. This went on for some time until a bell rang.

"Land ho!" someone yelled from above them.

"Land ho?" a few questioned, racing to the bow to take a look.

"Land ho!" several pirates exclaimed a moment before the crew began to scurry around like madmen. Pirates all over the ship climbed up the masts to adjust the rigging and sails while others scrambled above and below deck to ready the ship to drift closer to shore. Meanwhile, Maera and Theo went to the front of the boat to see.

Squinting their eyes against the bright sun, they saw an island ahead in the distance. As the ship sailed closer, little blue water dragons appeared. They jumped out of the water along the sides of the ship and then dove back into the water like dolphins do, riding the waves that the boat was making.

"Look, Maera!" Theo smiled.

"They look so friendly... and small," Maera noted. However, she also thought they looked cute, not that she'd admit that out loud. When they got as close to land as the captain dared to, Blight handed Maera and Theo real swords.

"Strap those on you two, you're both coming ashore," Blight instructed. Maera and Theo strapped the swords onto their waists, then followed Blight to a small boat hanging just over the side of the ship, held up by ropes. "Climb in, mateys!" Blight instructed.

"I'll go first," Maera said. She climbed in and then held out her hand to help Theo get in next. Ten other crew got in after, along with the captain. They were lowered to the water below before they unhooked the ropes, and the crew rowed them to shore. A small beach sat next to the sea cliffs.

"What is this place?" Theo questioned.

"This should be Emerald Island," Captain Willabee answered. "The crystal-clear freshwater pools have mermaids, the jungle has tiny dinosaurs, and the beach to the north has buried treasure."

"Why didn't we land at that beach?" Theo asked.

"The reefs there will sink the ship, laddie. Only a carouser would dare sail to that shore."

Maera tilted her head inquisitively. "What's a carouser?"

"Why, it be a pirate word for a reckless or crazy fool!" Willabee laughed. "The best way to get to the beach be through the jungle."

"Are the dinosaurs scary?" Theo inquired.

"Nay," Willabee rumbled with a crooked grin. "They be small and entirely friendly."

"Are there any monsters here?" Maera asked with a level of hope.

"Nay, lassie," he guffawed. "Not here."

Maera frowned, wishing that maybe just this once, something in Dream would remind her of home. A good scary rock giant would be perfect in a place like this.

Everyone got out and helped pull the little boat out of the water and onto the shore until the front of the rowboat ran aground. A few clouds were now starting to roll in, making the air nice and cool. Meanwhile, Captain Willabee led the way into the jungle ahead. Everyone used their swords to cut at the branches and vegetation in their way, clearing a path.

"Look!" Theo pointed excitedly. Everyone looked to see a herd of tiny, long-necked dinosaurs running by before disappearing into the brush the size of cats.

"Cute fellas, aren't they?" Blight chuckled.

"Very!" Theo replied. When no other dinosaurs appeared, the group pressed on, cutting their way deeper into the jungle. It was a lot of work, and Maera felt bored. In Nightmare, the jungle would have all kinds of monsters jumping at you, not like Dream.

If only I were in Nightmare, she thought as she smacked at a couple of vines and branches with her sword. *This would be much more dangerous... and fun.*

"Are we there yet?" Theo asked after a while.

"Does anyone hear any singing?" Blight inquired.

"Nay," everyone answered.

"Then we carry on, me hearties," Captain Willabee hollered back as he led the way forward. Maera looked up at the darkening sky, and her scowl turned into a smile. Clouds gathered, blotting out the blue and keeping the bright sun hidden.

"The skies here look kind of like Nightmare," Maera whispered to Theo with a big grin.

"What?" Theo asked. "Really?" He glanced up. "It just looks dark and cloudy to me."

"Exactly," Maera replied, then paused. "Captain?"

"Aye, lassie?"

"Is this island on the edge of Nightmare?" The idea that she was close to home made her happy.

"What? Nay, lassie! We be a good distance away," the captain retorted.

"Are you sure?" Maera pressed.

"Of course! Why, I charted the course meself!" he declared.

Finally, they reached the base of the mountain at the center of the island.

"Wait, do you hear that?" one of the crew asked. Everyone grew silent and listened. Birds suddenly took flight just before a rumbling noise cut through the silence. The rumbling got louder until the ground trembled.

"Shiver me timbers," one of the pirates whispered with fear.

"Earthquake!" Theo yelled.

"That be no earthquake," Blight stated darkly. "That be much worse. The dream is changing."

"What? How?" Theo demanded with growing concern.

"Your guess be as good as me own, lad," Blight said. He looked around and frowned. "I think... I think we be entering into a nightmare!"

"By golly, you're right," Captain Willabee agreed. "Though,

how that be even possible...." He shook his head. "This be Dream, not Nightmare." The captain looked at Maera and Theo. "Did you do this, mateys?"

Theo frowned. "No way!"

When they looked at Maera, she felt a pang of guilt. "I thought it would be nice to have some friends here like I do in Nightmare, but I didn't change anything. I can't," Maera told them. "My father is the only one who can create Wonders and new nightmares using the red sand and his staff." Though Maera didn't believe she had any power to change a dream, part of her was curious if she actually had. She questioned whether it was, in some way, her fault. She had been hoping for something familiar to appear, like the Wonders from Nightmare, right before things changed, thinking that Dream was just too pleasant. It was just too nice, too bright and happy, and she missed Nightmare.

"Strange," Willabee frowned. "This be strange indeed." The ground rumbled and shook even more.

"What do we do?" Theo panicked. "What about the treasure?" Suddenly, rocks tumbled down the mountain toward them.

"Never you mind that," Blight answered, "We be needing to get out of here." The mountain above began to break apart, revealing three huge giants made of rock and grass.

"Blimey, those be rock giants!" Willabee shouted.

"Blow me down," another pirate said in shock.

"Back to the ship, mateys!" The captain ordered before everyone ran.

Maera could only stare up at them, thrilled to see the impressive giants. "They're so handsome!"

"Maera!" Theo called after her, having spun around to see she wasn't following. One giant began to crash through the trees after the retreating pirates. The crew was already leaving her behind. "Maera, we need to go!" Theo remained, waiting for her, but she could see he was afraid.

"It's okay," Maera replied calmly. "They won't hurt me. I'm from Nightmare." Maera wanted to name these new giants, but to her surprise, they grabbed large boulders and hurled them at her and the others.

"Maera!" Theo screamed. "Run!"

She blinked at them in surprise until the closest one picked up another big rock, getting ready to throw it. "I don't understand." Maera frowned. *Maybe it's because I'm with the others that the giants are now attacking me along with them. Nightmares feed on fear, and Theo is clearly afraid.* "Don't be scared of them," Maera tried to explain, but another rock was tossed, and this time, it landed only a few feet away from where she stood.

"Maera!" Theo raced toward her. "Maera, we need to go, NOW!" He grabbed her hand, and together they ran after the crew. Another large rock flew by, crashing into the brush just ahead of them and causing more birds to fly up into the air from the disturbance. They raced through the jungle after the pirates. When they reached the beach where the cliff once was, Maera noticed it was now gone. Instead, more rock giants stood at the shore and began chasing after them. The crew quickly grabbed the boat and dragged it into the water, pushing it past the waves before they climbed inside and began to row quickly. Maera raced across the beach to catch up.

"Hurry, mateys!" Willabee beckoned. Blight and the captain reached out their hands, and together, they pulled Maera into the boat while Theo floated in from above. The crew rowed as fast as they could while the rock giants tossed large boulders at them. When they crashed down with a large splash, it rocked the boat. "Heave ho, me hearties!" he urged, and the pirates rowed faster while more rocks crashed into the water nearby.

The disturbance caused a flock of little water dragons to begin swimming away from the island. Several leaped through the air, then dove back into the water. More rocks were thrown at them, and one clipped one of the little dragons' wings. Maera felt bad about that.

"Oh no!" Theo reached out and scooped the little blue dragon up while everyone else kept rowing. When they reached the waiting ship, everyone scrambled to get the boat lifted toward the ship's deck. The moment they were aboard the ship again, the captain hurried to the back of the boat and stood by the stairs.

"Set them sails, mateys! Weigh anchor and hoist the mizzen!" Captain Willabee barked out to the crew. "We be needing to get far away from this blasted island before those cursed giants sink me ship and take us all down to Davy Jones's Locker! Blight!" he bellowed. "Grab the helm and steer me ship, I'm going to look over the maps. Emerald Island has to be somewhere close, and with it, we'll have more riches than we'll know what to do with."

"Aye, aye, captain," Blight and the crew all said before they ran around, pulling up the anchor, adjusting the sails, and thrusting large oars into the water to speedily get the ship turned around. It was a mad race to sail the ship away from the island.

Meanwhile, Theo tried helping the small water dragon. "Maera," he looked at her with pleading eyes. "Tell me you know how to fix this."

"Um," Maera frowned, "I can *try*." She sat next to Theo and let her hand hover over the small dragon's broken wing. "Little dragon, close your eyes and remember how it felt to have your wing whole and working. Imagine it being strong." She ran her hand over the dragon's wing. By the second time she ran her hand over it, the wing had healed.

"You did it!" Theo exclaimed with joy. "All right, little fella, you're all better now." Theo stood and took the dragon to the side of the ship. He held out his arms and bounced the dragon up and down.

"Go on," he urged. "Just spread your wings and fly. You can do it." The dragon squawked and opened his little wings. Suddenly, the dragon flew. Maera grinned, and Theo looked delighted when it landed back in the water and joined its family as they leaped out of the water next to the boat, landing back into the water with a splash. The dragons did this for a while, following the ship, and then, one by one, they disappeared under the water completely.

"They're going home," Theo smiled.

CHAPTER

TEN

Maera and Theo leaned against the ship's railing, looking out at the big blue sea. Maera missed her home. "What's your home like?" Maera inquired, hoping Theo could take her mind off it.

"Mine?" Theo blinked, and Maera nodded. "It's a two-story house with a front porch. My bedroom is upstairs, along with my sister's and older brother's. Well, it was. When I got sicker, I couldn't get up the stairs anymore, so my parents moved me into the room downstairs. It used to be my dad's office, but now it's just a boring bedroom. All my posters and things are still upstairs in my other room. I really miss it," Theo said. "It's been a long time since I got to sleep upstairs. I suppose it's been a while since I've been home, too."

The last statement surprised Maera. "So, you're still at the hospital in the Waking World?"

Theo nodded. It now made sense that he was still in the strange gown. Everyone wore one anytime she'd visited the Crumbling Hospital.

"Oh!" Theo exclaimed, snapping her attention back to the

present. "That's right! Maera, I have to *tell* you something... something *crazy*."

"What is it?" Maera asked.

"There's this room in the pediatric ward of the hospital. That's where all the children like me are treated. The room is the one next to mine. Everyone on that floor says it's the ghost girl's room. There's this grumpy old man who visits her every couple of days. My friend Connor said she's been in there for a long time. He's been at the hospital off and on for two years because he has some immune disease, and he said that she was there even longer than him!"

She perked up with interest. "A ghost girl? Like a real ghost? Did you see her? Does she look like a ghost? Are there really ghosts in the Waking World, too? I thought they only existed in Nightmare."

"I think there are ghosts," Theo frowned in thought. "I haven't seen any, though."

"So you didn't see if she was actually a ghost?" Maera asked.

"No one ever gets too close to that room. They're all scared of it."

Confused, her brows knit together. "Then how do you know if she's a ghost?"

"Sandra said she swore she saw her before, and so did Tommy," Theo replied. "Then they said they had scary dreams about her wandering through the hospital, except I thought it was silly talk," he rolled his eyes. "Why would a ghost need to stay at the hospital? The hospital is for people, not ghosts. But then Billy dared me to go into the room when I said I wasn't scared. The old man who visited that room had already left for the day, and Tommy said if I went in there, he'd give me his chocolate pudding. So, to prove them wrong, I went inside."

"And...?" Maera pressed.

"*And* the girl in that room looked just like you—the same curly brown hair and everything!"

"That's weird," Maera frowned. "Why would someone look like me? I was born in Nightmare."

"I don't know, but everyone is afraid of the ghost girl in room 311. Only, when I went into the room and saw her, she wasn't a ghost. She was just asleep. She didn't even look scary, and I got chocolate pudding out of it," Theo supplied with a grin.

"Room 311?" Maera whispered. *That's weird*, Maera thought. *311 is the number scratched on my bedroom door in the castle.* Maera's lips tugged downward. *Why would that be there? Why would the girl in the Waking World look like me?*

"Want me to see if I can find out who she is?" Theo offered.

"Um... maybe?"

Maera was quiet for a long time after that. The clouds followed them, making the water rougher, a perfect representation of her troubled thoughts, though she wasn't entirely aware of this. Glancing down at the sea, Maera wasn't sure, but she thought she saw something moving every so often underneath the surface—something large and gray, but then it would disappear for a while, and she thought maybe her mind was playing tricks on her. Something about it ate at the back of her brain... a memory, perhaps. No matter how hard she tried to recall what it was, she couldn't. For as long as she'd been in Nightmare, she didn't ever remember being on the ocean.

The ship rocked in the waves, and Maera stumbled, reaching out to hold onto the ship. A couple of crew members chuckled.

"Don't worry, lass," one said as he adjusted the ropes tied to the side of the ship. "You'll get your sea legs soon enough. This storm will make a real pirate out of you." They carried on with their work, and Maera hung onto the rail.

"Do you think we'll come across any other pirates?" Theo asked after a while, holding on just as tightly to the railing as the ship rocked from the growing waves. The ocean was getting a little choppier. "What if other pirates got to the treasure?"

"I guess it's possible," Maera replied. "The pirates in Nightmare like to attack other ships and take whatever treasures they can find on board, or so I've heard. I've never been on any of the ships, so I don't know for sure."

The water grew rougher, and the clouds above darkened. Lightning flashed before it rained, and the wind picked up. Captain Willabee reappeared from his cabin to take over steering the ship. "Trim the sails, lads! Tighten the rigging and batten down the hatches! We be heading into a storm!"

Crew members climbed the ropes and began adjusting the big white sails. Others began securing the cargo and readying the ship for the oncoming storm. Seeing the darkening skies and the larger waves, Maera thought this felt more like Nightmare than Dream.

Then a bell rang, and someone in the crow's nest above hailed, "Sail, ho! Ship Ahoy!"

"What does that mean?" Theo inquired from where he stood by the railing.

"It means a ship's been spotted," one of the crew tossed out before racing off.

"I need me spyglass," Willabee announced as he gripped the wheel, then rang a golden bell.

The crew went wild as they got busy while Blight took over the helm. Willabee thumped along with his peg leg toward the very back of the boat to look at the oncoming ship. Maera and Theo raced up the steps, following after him. Theo's legs *clacked* against the wooden deck, much like the captain's. Leaning against the taffrail, Willabee extended a small gold telescope.

Maera tried squinting her eyes, but with the wind, the waves, and the oncoming storm, she couldn't see anything. The ship was too far away to get a proper look. "Captain, what is it? Is it really another ship?" Maera asked, dying with curiosity.

"Yes, and by the look of her, lassie, me thinks it be a pirate ship." Willabee handed the spyglass to Maera. Through it, she saw a tiny ship in the distance. It was dark with black sails. She handed it to Theo, who took a look next.

"Are ships usually dark with black sails here?" Theo asked.

"Nay, laddie. Them bilge-sucking blokes be the worst of the worst—scum of the ocean, bottom of the barrel, those pirates. Cutthroats."

Willabee took back the telescope and plunked across the back upper deck to look out at his crew. "Reef them sails, me hearties! These pirates want to give chase. Let's show them what we be made of!" Willabee thumped toward the helm, taking over for Blight. Blight went to the stern and looked out.

"Now they be hoisting their Jolly Rodger," Blight warned.

"They have, have they?" Captain Willabee laughed.

"What's a Jolly Rodger?" Maera asked Blight.

"Why it be their flag, lassie," he answered while the captain barked, "Hoist the colors!"

The crew all roared in reply, "Hoist the colors," and soon, their flag rose up the mast. It was red with a skull on it. The moment the red flag unfurled, flapping in the wind, the crew sang a pirate's sea chanty while they worked.

"Can't we just outrun them?" Theo inquired nervously.

The pirate captain laughed heartily. "Nay, lad! We be pirates! We'll fight! I'll be bringing a spring upon her now." Willabee then gripped the wheel and spun it hard. The ship lurched as it turned. Soon, everyone was getting ready for the battle ahead. "Ready the chase guns!" he hollered.

When they got closer to the other ship, crew members fired two cannons from the front of the ship. However, the cannon balls both splashed into the water, not even close to the other ship. They were still too far away, giving the crew time to ready the cannons again. Then, with loud booms, they fired the cannons again, only this time, they splashed just in front of the other ship. In return, the other ship fired their cannons, which splashed a couple of yards away from Willabee's prow.

"Aim for their masts, mateys!" the captain instructed. "Slow these scurvy dogs down and take out their sails!"

"Aye, aye, captain!" the crew replied. The crew fired again. This time, they hit the front mast, causing it to snap and fall.

"Jolly good!" Willabee laughed. "We be pulling in closer now." He turned the wheel moments before the other ship fired more cannons, missing them by a hair.

Theo looked scared, but Maera felt excited. Willabee manned the helm, turning the ship to expose the broadside.

"Fire the big guns!" Willabee barked. "Give them a little scare!"

"Aye, aye, captain!" several pirates hollered, then went below deck to give the orders.

"Fire in the hole!" crewmembers cried from below deck. As the ship turned, all the cannons on the deck below fired along the right side. Some of the cannonballs hit the water near the other ship, sending water shooting into the air. A few struck the enemy ship itself, leaving large holes in the hull, and the crew all cheered, "Yo ho, ho!"

The captain turned the ship again when the enemy fired their cannons in return. Maera and Theo ducked when one blasted through the railing, sending wood flying in all directions.

"Get ready, me hearties!" Willabee called out. "No prey, no plunder!"

"Aye, aye, captain! No prey, no plunder!" the crew yelled in unison.

When they were close enough to the other ship, they ran right alongside it, and the crew used ropes to swing across the gap and land on the other ship's deck. Others tossed ropes with grappling hooks to crawl across the moment the rope was secured. Then the real fight began. The pirates on the other ship were rough, dirty, and mean-looking. Some had horrible scars. Others were missing a finger or an eye and wearing an eyepatch. Quite a few had yellow teeth and looked like they could really use a bath. They all wore red or black clothes, making them look even more intimidating.

"Draw your swords, scallywags," Blight shouted at Maera and Theo. "We be fighting to the death!"

"Uh," Theo paled, "I don't want to die."

"Come on," Maera smiled, drawing her sword. "This is going to be fun!"

"Aaaaarrrrrgggghhhh!" a mean enemy pirate growled, swinging aboard their ship and drawing his sword. A couple of other pirates in red and black did the same, so Maera jumped right into the fray. Theo drew his sword, and together, they fought some of these cutthroat pirates alongside a couple of fellow crewmembers.

The sound of swords clanging was loud. The storm unleashed sheets of rain, and the waves tossed both vessels up and down. A few times, Theo slipped, and Maera helped fend off the pirates, trying to cut them down until he could get back up. Eventually, Theo flew, using that to his advantage while he sliced and slashed at the enemy pirates. Some of Willabee's crew knocked pirates into the rough waves. Others were knocked out cold, slumping to the deck. A few were tied up to the masts of the other ship. After a while, it looked like Willabee's crew was winning.

A loud splash distracted Maera from the fight, and she looked in time to see a serpent-like tail disappear under the water.

"What's that?" she gasped. The pirate she was fighting turned, as did Theo and the hairy pirate he fought. The choppy, dark water showed nothing at first, but then the head of a giant sea dragon breached the surface. It had two tentacles on its lip, looking like a mustache, and several smaller ones under its chin. As it rose out of the water, it looked more like a serpent than a dragon. It was a strange grayish-green color and only had two arms with sharp claws. The rest of it was long with thin spikes along its back. For a second, it looked familiar, but the memory was gone in a flash, and Maera shook her head.

"The Mad Dragon," whispered the dark-haired pirate who'd been fighting Maera.

"Shiver me timbers," the hairy pirate who'd been fighting Theo said in fear. "It will sink our ships and send us to our graves!"

"We need to get out of here!" Maera's enemy declared. A large splash rocked the ship, and Maera stumbled, trying not to fall.

"The Mad Dragon!" another pirate cried out. Suddenly, everyone scrambled. The enemy pirates quickly left and returned to their own ship. Willabee's crew came back aboard their boat. With a loud shriek, the dragon shot out of the ocean entirely, flying up overhead. Water dripped down upon them from the underbelly while the dragon arched over the two ships to dive into the sea on the other side.

It's HUGE! And... strangely familiar.

"Everyone to their stations! All hands on deck and heave ho!" Willabee thundered. "We must sail like the wind, or the Mad Dragon will be our doom, taking us down to Davy Jones's locker!"

Everyone worked quickly while Captain Willabee manned the helm, steering them away from the other ship with the black sails. The Mad Dragon surfaced again, landing on the other boat, and wood splintered in all directions. The pirates on that ship screamed and yelled, but it was too late. The Mad Dragon chomped at the masts and used its large body to break apart the boat. In moments, the ship was sinking.

"Hurry, lads! Adjust the rigging and sails. We must capture as much wind as we can and get out of here!" Willabee barked.

"Aye, aye, captain!" the crew hailed and began desperately untying the ropes and sails as everyone scrambled to flee from the Mad Dragon.

As the dragon leaped from the wreckage of the other ship and made a spectacular landing with a deafening splash, Theo whispered in awed fear. "We're going to die, aren't we?"

"If you die in a dream, you'll just wake up," Maera assured him while they clung to the railing of the ship in the rough seas.

"Oh yeah," Theo sighed in relief.

Eventually, the ship was too far away to see over the rough seas. The ship tossed about in the ocean as the water got rougher, and the storm was in full swing. Waves splashed over the sides, and Maera lost her hold on the ship's railing.

"Watch out, mateys!" Willabee warned as water splashed across the deck. "Hang on tight, or you be feeding the fish tonight!"

"Maera!" Theo's desperate attempts to reach for her amid the chaos were thwarted as the relentless seawater rushed up over the deck and swept her away toward the other side of the ship. She bumped up against the rail and grabbed onto it. The ship rode the crest of yet another wave, careening down the other side and jolting forward with thrilling force. As the boat rocked violently, waves crashed over the sides and engulfed Theo, drenching him from head to toe and sending him sliding across the ship. Maera reached out, grabbing Theo's hand, but it was too wet and slippery, and she lost his grip.

"Maera!" Theo called out.

"Theo!" Maera screamed, but he tumbled overboard where the cannon had damaged part of the railing. "Theo!" Maera cried, getting to her feet. She rushed over, scanning the choppy water to catch a glimpse of him.

"Man overboard!" Maera heard the person in the crow's nest shout just as she noticed the back of the Mad Dragon break the surface, swimming toward their ship... and Theo.

"Hang on, Theo!" Maera hollered.

"Grab the rope and haul him back, mateys!" Willabee ordered, but the Mad Dragon had just spotted Theo.

"Theo! Look out!" Maera warned.

Theo turned to see the dragon, fear etching itself across his face. The serpent rose in the sea, poised to leap into the air and land on Theo. Blight tossed a rope, but it caught in the wind and landed too far from where Theo bobbed in the water. Maera grabbed hold of another rope and swiftly flung it toward her friend. The dragon breached the surface, rising out of the water and arching its body into another dive, approaching Theo with a ravenous hunger in its glowing green eyes.

"Theo!" Maera didn't think. She jumped overboard in haste to help her friend. Suddenly, her wings sprouted, and she flew toward Theo faster than she knew was possible. She reached him just as the giant serpent opened its mouth and landed, swallowing the two friends in its massive jaws. Theo disappeared in the nick of time, right before the monster snapped its jaws closed.

CHAPTER

ELEVEN

Maera woke in her bedroom, lying on top of her dark purple blanket. The dragon had sent her home to the obsidian castle in Nightmare. When she got out of bed, she ran to the door and frowned when she saw the 311, remembering what Theo had said.

Bones stood outside her room. "You're back," the skeleton knight in armor rattled. "Your father asked that you see him right away."

Maera followed Bones to the throne room, marching up to the platform where her father sat on his throne.

"Where have you been?" the king demanded.

"Well, I was in Dream with a group of pirates. Then, I ended up back in Nightmare," Maera answered.

"Why were you in Dream?"

"Theo wanted to go there," Maera toed the ground.

"Theo, the Sleeper?"

"Yes," Maera reluctantly answered.

"I thought I forbade you to see him."

She said nothing.

"Maera, I *told* you to stay away from him," he said with disap-

130

pointment. "You said you wouldn't interfere with any more nightmares."

"Except he came and found *me*," Maera argued. "If it's not allowed, how come he remembers me when he comes back here?"

"Most people remember their nightmares better than their dreams. Still, it would've been best if you hadn't gone with him. The Land of Dreams is changing, and the borders of Nightmare have shifted. This Sleeper is strong to be able to do that, so I don't want you near that boy from now on."

"But Father, Theo's my *friend*."

"No 'buts,' and no going into Dream. If you get into trouble there, I can't help you." He paused, giving her a hard look. "I see you've died again."

"One of your Wonders caused it this time, but that was after the rock giants you created had attacked me," Maera huffed, crossing her arms.

"Rock giants?" the king asked, looking puzzled. "I never created any rock giants."

Maera frowned. "You didn't?"

The king shook his head, and she saw a flash of concern cross his sharp features for a moment before it was gone.

"What about the Mad Dragon?" she asked next, feeling a little troubled that the Wonders were turning on her.

"Oh, the Mad Dragon chased the Sleeper, not you," he waved his hand dismissively, but then he leaned forward. "Why did you interfere?"

"I...." Maera deflated. "I wanted to help my friend, Theo."

"This Theo is a bad influence," the king stated. "You've been breaking all the rules I've set since you and he met, so from now on, you're forbidden from ever seeing him again."

"Father, no!"

"I'm not finished!" he barked, then in a calmer voice, continued. "I'm grounding you, Maera. You are to remain here in the castle where it's safe. Alessandra told me you revealed to the boy that he could alter his dreams. Now he's started changing things. Then you went back to Dream after I told you not to. Next, you'll be visiting the Roads of Wreckage... or worse, the lost dreams or nightmares that are dissolving into nothingness. You're forbidden from seeing Theo."

"Why?" Maera demanded. "Why can't I be friends with him? I said I wouldn't interfere with his nightmares, and I haven't–he's the one who found me! I just want to be a part of someone's nightmare for once. What am I going to do locked up in the castle?"

"Perhaps you should think more about who and what you are to Nightmare," he suggested.

"The last time I was grounded, I *tried* finding my purpose," she complained with frustration. "I really did. I've been here for so long, and I'm the *only* Wonder who doesn't have one! Why? Why don't I have one? It isn't fair."

"Because you're special," her father replied patiently. "You're my Night Maera. You don't have to have a purpose like the others. Don't you want me to keep you safe? Don't you want me to protect you from harm? The world is a dangerous place, Maera; I worry that this Theo is changing too many things here. I'm not sure you're prepared to face the consequences that could follow."

"Theo wouldn't hurt me," Maera argued.

"Maybe not on purpose," the king replied. "What if by changing his nightmares or dreams, he makes Hagetha disappear? Or Colossal? Won't you miss your friends if he did? What if he causes you to disappear?"

"He wouldn't," Maera shook her head. *At least, I don't think so.*

"I can see that you're not so sure about that. He doesn't see things the way you do. He wants to destroy Nightmare, which is something I can't allow. Stay away from that boy, Maera. Do you understand me?"

Maera frowned at her father. She felt he was being unfair. Yet, if Theo could change the dreams, she also didn't want her friends to disappear.

"Well?" he asked.

Feeling conflicted, she nodded.

"Good. Now, go to your room," her father ordered.

"But—"

"No 'buts.' I'm doing this for your protection, daughter. Do as you're told."

Maera turned to leave but then stopped and looked back. "Why does my room have 311 on it?" Bones, who had begun escorting her out of the throne room, stopped short.

The king looked genuinely surprised. "What?"

"My door, why is the number 311 scratched onto it?" Maera asked again.

Her father frowned. "You don't know?"

"No."

Her father nodded. "It appeared the day you arrived in Nightmare."

"It appeared the day I was born?"

"Yes...," the king answered mysteriously. "I'm certain that it has to do with your purpose."

"Really?" *So, I* do *have a purpose!* "Why didn't you tell me sooner?" Maera cried, feeling both upset that he'd known while also feeling excited to have another clue to help her search.

"Because everyone here in Nightmare must find their path, whether it's Sleepers who need nightmares to help them learn and grow, or Wonders who are born here to play the roles they were born to play. Only a Wonder knows what their purpose is. Only a Sleeper can find the meaning behind their dreams or nightmares."

"Oh. You... you can't just tell me? Aren't you the king?"

"When you're ready, you'll learn the truth," the king replied.

"Meanwhile, go to your room and think about the importance of following the rules. Perhaps you might reflect upon things and learn a lesson from all of this."

What lesson could she learn? She wanted to be friends with Theo, but by being friends, she risked losing her friends in Nightmare. She also wanted to find out why she'd been born in Nightmare... yet nothing she'd learned so far had helped her figure that out.

Unsure of what else to do, Maera trailed after Bones, who took her back to her room. When she got there, she reached out and touched the numbers, wishing they'd reveal their secret—hoping they'd help her learn her purpose.

DAYS PASSED, turning into weeks, then weeks turned into one month, going on two, and Maera had decided to spend the time trying to figure out how to unlock her purpose. When she wasn't stuck inside the large castle, she tailed after the witches on their hunts, but that didn't inspire any new ideas. So, she hung out with the clowns in the Carnival of Creeps, but all they ever liked to do was prank Sleepers or play dangerous games that resulted in her dying and ending back in her room. Occasionally, she spent the day with Colossal, but he was of no help either, and sadly, neither was Stinky, Grunt, nor Groan.

Sulking, Maera walked through the various rooms and halls of the castle, hoping to find more clues etched onto the doors or walls. Meanwhile, Alessandra and Bones kept her company.

Out of hope and ideas, Maera would ask her father if any new nightmares or Wonders were born during mealtimes, wanting to hear the latest stories. In return, she'd tell him about the days that she'd filled with her search for answers. He never volunteered any new information that could help her, but occasionally, he'd invite her to the balcony above his throne to watch whenever he made new nightmares. Unfortunately, this only reminded her that, unlike the other Wonders, she still didn't know where she fit in within Nightmare. For the first time in her life, she was no longer thrilled to see the new nightmares scare Sleepers... instead, it made her feel sad.

Sometimes, when Maera hung out in her room, she'd look out her window and think about Theo. She hoped he was doing okay in the Waking World. She often wondered about that ghost girl he'd mentioned. It was so weird that someone in the Waking World would look just like her. She pondered on whether there were others in the Waking World who looked like the Queen of Dreams or like her father, the King of Nightmares. What if there were people that looked like Sinda? Or Hagetha? Then she'd imagine what those Sleepers would be like in the Waking World. She doubted she'd ever know and figured if she ever saw Theo again, she would ask him.

"I wonder if he's had any new nightmares," she contemplated aloud to her little bat friend. She was sitting by her opened bedroom window when the little creature had come by to visit.

Unlike most creatures in Nightmare, the little bat was soft, and she scratched its round, little belly while it hung upside down from her finger, stretching out its leathery wings. Eventually, it fluttered off. With a sigh, she closed the pane as the wind turned chilly.

Looking out, she could only see parts of Nightmare from here: the Roads of Wreckage and the Haunted Plains. She frowned at the distant hills full of gravestones and again thought about Theo. From this view, she hadn't seen him flying, nor had she seen him while she'd been out adventuring in her search for clues. She missed her friend and considered the chance he was still in the hospital or if he'd finally been able to go home and sleep in his room upstairs, which he said he missed.

Later that night, Maera lay in her bed wondering if or when she'd ever get to be a part of a nightmare like the other Wonders when she heard a strange tapping at her window. Sitting up, she looked out, and to her surprise, she saw Theo floating just outside.

"Theo?" she whispered and slid out of bed, then hurried over to open the window.

"I finally found you!" he said excitedly and flew right in.

"Shhh," she hushed, looking toward her door nervously. "I'm not supposed to see you anymore. My father said you're a bad influence."

"Me?" He looked surprised and landed. Immediately, she noticed he had a strange contraption strapped to his leg.

"What's that?" She pointed.

"A prosthetic leg," Theo replied. "Do...." He frowned. "Do you think it's ugly?"

"No! It's so much fancier than the wooden one Captain Will-abee got for you," Maera replied and was rewarded with a smile.

"It's taken me months to learn how to use it." Theo's smile suddenly vanished. "Maera, I had to find you. Before I left the hospital, I was caught in the room next door to mine, 311, and that old, cranky man came in. He was angry at first, thinking that I was playing games. He knew the other children called her ghost girl. But then I said I was only visiting that room because the girl in there looked lonely. After that, he was okay with me visiting. He said that she was in a coma and that she'd been asleep for almost three years."

"A coma?" Maera asked.

"Yes. She was in a bad accident and never woke up," Theo replied. "The old man is her grandfather. He said her parents died in the accident. That's why he is so sad. His daughter was the girl's mom. He also said that if she doesn't wake up soon, they're going to pull her plugs. Isn't that awful?" She nodded.

"How did you find me?" Maera questioned, wanting to change the subject. For some reason, talking about this girl bothered her.

"Oh, I've been looking all over for you. I've been coming to Nightmare a lot but haven't seen you around."

"I guess lately I haven't left the castle much." She'd been pouting for days after coming up empty-handed with no new clues about why she'd been born in Nightmare.

"Maybe that's why," Theo said thoughtfully.

"But how did you find me *here*?" Maera asked.

"I've been looking for you for weeks! When I couldn't find you, I started looking around the castle as soon as the coast was clear. I've looked in all the windows the last several times I came to Nightmare until I had to wake up."

"How? I mean, if you're coming to Nightmare, aren't you scared? How are you getting away?"

"Well, I listened to what you said that one time... you know, about changing things? I've gotten better at changing my dreams! And you're right! The zombies aren't so bad when you get to know them. Stinky is really cool. Did you know he knows how to skip stones across the water? And Fleshy knows how to wrestle the crocodiles. Grunt and Groan can charm the snakes, and I even got to pet one!" Theo grinned. "Doc doesn't scare me anymore, either; he's my friend now. He plays video games in his office on the second floor, and he lets me play sometimes. So, whenever I have a nightmare and see him or the zombies, I can change the dream. Then I fly around to look for you. It's taken me a while, but when I didn't see you out there, I started looking around the castle and finally found the room with you in it!"

"Now what?" Maera asked. "I'm not supposed to hang out with you anymore."

"Can't we fly out and go somewhere they won't find us?" Theo questioned. "Like we've done before?"

"I... I guess, but I have to stay in Nightmare this time."

"Oh," Theo's face fell. "Is there anywhere we can go in Nightmare, then?"

"Well... there is this one place I know that hardly anyone goes, where only Sleepers usually visit," Maera said. "Few Wonders are found there."

"Where's that?" Theo asked.

"A place I'm not supposed to go–The Roads of Wreckage."

"That sounds scary." Theo looked skeptical. "Can't we go to that place with the skeleton unicorns?"

"Um, that's near the forgotten nightmares. I'm not supposed to go there anymore. Sometimes those places just disappear."

"I guess that leaves the Roads of Wreckage, then. Can you fly?" Theo asked.

"I think so." She'd been practicing over the weeks. With a little concentration, her wings sprouted, and she felt that lifting into the air and flying was getting easier to control.

"Perfect! Let's go!" Theo jumped up to the ledge of her open window and then fell out. Maera went over to find him floating just outside. Maera climbed up and gave her wings a couple of test flaps before she jumped out. She dropped a little, but soon, her wings spread, and she was flying.

"Where is it?" Theo inquired.

"This way." Maera led the way toward the Haunted Plains.

"This place is way creepy!" Theo hollered when they passed over hundreds of gravestones. A few skeletons and zombies were chasing various Sleepers while several ghosts wandered around. Other Sleepers screamed from the graves they found themselves buried in.

"What's that sound?" Theo questioned.

"Oh, probably some of the Sleepers underground."

"There are people buried *alive* down there?" Theo balked, and Maera grinned, happy to be hanging out with her friend again.

"Some," she replied. "Those are the boring Sleepers. They just lay in a coffin underground and yell nonstop. I like watching the Sleepers that get chased by the ghosts, skeletons, or zombies better."

"You're so strange," Theo shook his head, but then a small smile spread across his face.

She banked to the right, heading toward the tangle of roads. Some of them were city roads that sat higher up than others, like overpasses, whereas others were in a country setting, and a few were as wide as eight lanes! Past those were a handful that were quieter streets with as little as two lanes, and that's the direction Maera headed. As she soared over some, she noticed a couple of the busier ones had zombies, so Maera steered clear of those. She didn't want them running and telling on her, so she flew to the unpopulated area, landing on one road where it was dark, quiet, and raining. Seeing it from the ground, her stomach twisted.

"What's wrong?" Theo inquired as she anxiously looked around.

"I... I don't know. I've never been here before, but it feels like I have for some reason," Maera confessed before she took a step onto the wet road.

"Look out!" Theo pushed her out of the way just as a truck appeared, honking at them as it raced by. They managed to dodge it just in time. "That was close," Theo panted with wide eyes as he sat on the wet grass on the side of the road. "You didn't tell me that cars and trucks can appear out of nowhere!"

"I didn't know," Maera replied, feeling just as surprised. "This is my first time coming to this part of Nightmare. Like I told you, I'm not supposed to be here."

"Let's stick to the sides of the road then," Theo suggested. "So, what have you been doing since I saw you last?"

"Um… not much. At first, I was grounded, so I stayed close to home," Maera explained. "Then, for a while, I tried looking for clues to help me discover my purpose."

"Did you find any?"

"No," she replied, pulling up little blades of wet grass and tossing them toward the road, but the truck never reappeared.

"So… you got in trouble for going to Dream?" Theo asked after a moment.

"Yeah."

"That sucks," he frowned, and then he stood up. "I get in trouble sometimes, too."

"You do?" Maera glanced over at him as he held out his hand. Taking it, he helped her up.

"Yep. Once, I was grounded for a whole week!"

"Why?" Maera asked before they started walking alongside the road.

"I got into a fight at school. Bradly is a bit of a bully. He kept calling me 'cancer kid' when I was going through chemotherapy. After I lost all my hair, he picked on me. That was before I was too sick to go to school. One day, when he spilled my lunch, I hit him. I was just so angry, and he didn't see it coming. Then he hit me, and I got a black eye. I was scared he'd keep hitting me, but then a teacher pulled him off me, and we both were sent home. My mom grounded me with no TV or video games for a whole week."

"But he was bullying you," Maera argued. *It doesn't seem fair at all.*

"I know. My dad said that Bradly had it coming, but my mom didn't want me to act out in violence. I told my mom I'd tried talking to Bradly first, but it only made it worse. He called me names and said I was just a scared little girl, too weak to fight him… that I was too sick—that I was practically no different from a baby."

"You should have hit him again," Maera grumbled. "He sounds like a jerk face."

"Except he's bigger than me," Theo argued as though that were a good enough answer. "If the teachers hadn't come, he'd have kicked my butt!"

"So, he kept picking on you after that?"

"Well, after that, I got sicker and haven't been back to school since. I have to do school at home now. Truthfully, I'm a little scared to go back," Theo confessed. "I grew out my hair since then... and the doctors said they didn't find any more cancer, so my mom said I'll be able to go back to school soon, but what if Bradly teases me because of my leg?"

"Theo, you fought *pirates*. I bet you can face Bradly," Maera said confidently.

"You think?" Theo frowned, looking uncertain.

"I think you're braver than you know," Maera replied. "You'd have to be after losing your hair and getting sick. You beat cancer, and you could probably beat Bradly, too."

"Hmmm," was all Theo said. They walked for a while longer. "You make me feel brave," he quietly admitted after a while. "Ever since I met you here in Nightmare, you make me feel like I can do anything."

"You can," Maera told him. "Especially in the Land of Dreams."

"We're friends, right?" Theo asked.

"Definitely," Maera smiled.

"Cool." He looked around. It was pretty dark here. The rain obscured any light, making it seem even darker. The quiet was almost creepy, perfect for Nightmare, but it left Maera feeling unsettled.

"Why are you forbidden from coming here?" Theo questioned after a minute. "It seems kind of boring."

"My father never said. He just told me I shouldn't come to this part of Nightmare." They reached a crossroads. There was a stop sign, but no cars were coming. However, the moment Maera stepped onto the pavement to cross, a car appeared idling at the stop sign. Maera watched while it rolled forward... when suddenly a truck came out of nowhere and fast, plowing right through the other stop sign and causing Maera and Theo to jump.

She watched as the truck tires screeched, breaking too late and filling the air with the stench of burnt rubber. The sound of the crash was so loud it was deafening, and Maera immediately felt very scared. The truck smashed into the other car, causing it to spin around before flipping over and rolling three times until it stopped. The car now lay upside down with smoke coming out of it, hissing as it continued to rain.

"Whoa! That was crazy!" Theo shouted when everything went still, grabbing both sides of his head in shock. "Do you think the Sleepers woke up before they ran into each other?" he asked. "Maera?"

Maera froze, staring at the car with the three people still inside.

"Maera?" Theo called out again.

Maera, as if in a daze, walked toward the car. When she looked through the back window, she was suddenly transported to the backseat. She was startled to find herself stuck upside down, and the seatbelt wouldn't come undone despite her efforts to push the button to free herself.

I'm trapped! she thought in terror. She hated feeling trapped. Two grown-ups were unmoving in the front seat. They looked like they'd gone to sleep. She didn't like being in the car like this and couldn't understand why the people in front weren't disappearing.

"Maera!" Theo ran toward the car.

"Theo!" Maera screamed. It was the first time she'd ever been truly afraid in Nightmare. "Theo, I can't get out! I can't get out!" She was panicking.

"Hold on!" Theo yelled. "I'll help you."

"Hurry! Please hurry, Theo!" she cried. Tears filled her eyes as she pulled on the seatbelt. She kept pushing the button, but the seatbelt wouldn't let her go. Theo came over with a sharp piece of metal.

"I'll get you out," he promised as he crawled through the broken window to reach her.

"Don't leave me here, Theo," Maera begged. "Please get me out. I don't like this."

"Don't worry, I'm going to help you." Theo started sawing the strap of the seatbelt with the piece of metal. It took a while, but he eventually cut it, and Maera dropped out. Theo backed away from the car and then helped pull her out through the window. The moment they stepped onto the grass, the cars completely disappeared. The two of them were alone once more, and the street was now as quiet as the dead outside of the *pitter-patter* of rain. Maera took several deep breaths.

"I thought nightmares don't hurt you," Theo remarked.

"Th… they don't. They're not supposed to," Maera replied, wiping away her tears. "Thanks for saving me," she sniffled. She couldn't ignore the disturbing feeling that this was the first time she felt afraid in Nightmare.

Theo hugged her. "It's okay now."

"I want to get out of this place," Maera told him, feeling shaken, and then stepped away from him. "I don't like it here."

"Okay," Theo replied. "Let's go."

CHAPTER

TWELVE

Maera and Theo walked away from the Roads of Wreckage. However, before they got too far, the King of Nightmare stepped out of the shadows, holding his large staff and looking very angry.

"Father...."

"I told you never to come here," he thundered. Then he glanced at Theo, scrutinizing him. "I also forbade you to see this Sleeper again."

"Don't yell at her!" Theo warned, bravely stepping in between the King of Nightmares and Maera. "It was *my* fault. *I* found her in the castle and asked her to come with me."

"Maera still chose to leave, though, didn't she?" the king pointed out. "And then came here—the one place I asked her never to go."

"She wouldn't have come here if you'd just let her come with me to Dream!" Theo fired back. "Why are you keeping her away from me? She's my friend!"

"Watch your tone, boy, before I send you far from here, and you'll never see her again!" the king roared.

"Father, no," Maera cut in.

"Are you even her real dad? Who are you to tell her what to do?" Theo dared to ask, surprising the king.

Her father frowned. "*I* am the King of Nightmares, boy," her father announced icily. "I am the father of fears and bringer of chaos. I am the shadows and the darkness. I am the keeper of things that go bump in the night. Without me, dreams could not exist. Who are *you* to speak to *me* that way?"

"I'm Theo Wenrick, and I'm Maera's friend," Theo replied boldly.

"Those who live here aren't *friends* with Sleepers such as you," the king tossed back.

"But he *is* my friend," Maera argued.

"And *he* has been running from his nightmares, and *you*, my daughter, have helped him escape them. Time is running out, and certain lessons have yet to be learned. No more distractions. You're coming home right this instant. Say goodbye to your friend, Maera. This is the last time you'll see him here."

"No!" Theo protested.

"But Father...."

"Say goodbye!" her father ordered firmly. Maera slowly turned, seeing Theo's sad face.

"I'm sorry, Theo. I have to go." At that, her father took her hand, leading her toward the shadows.

"No! You can't!" Theo shouted after them. "Maera!" He limped toward the shadows, but before he could reach them, the king tapped his staff. Suddenly, a large, freckled boy stood between them and Theo.

"It's time to face your fears, boy," the king said before turning away and tugging Maera after him.

"Bradly," Theo frowned and backed away from the freckled boy. Meanwhile, Bradly pounded a fist into his hand and walked toward Theo with a sneer. He was taller than Theo by a few inches and was heavyset, wider than Theo by a good many inches.

"Look, it's Theo, the little *girl*," Bradly jeered, "I'm going to pay you back for hitting me, cancer boy. No one hits me and gets away with it." Theo took a step back, and Bradly laughed. "Oh, and look! You lost your leg. Do you actually think you can run from me? With that?" Bradly pointed to Theo's prosthetic leg a second before Theo took another step.

"This is only a nightmare," Theo chanted as he continued to back away from the bully. "Just a nightmare." Theo lifted into the air, ready to fly away, but Bradly morphed into a large red serpent with black wings and sharp claws, though his face still looked the same aside from the sharp teeth inside his mouth and the snake tongue that flicked the air.

"Not so fast, cancer boy," Bradly hissed before he took off and flew after Theo. He chased Theo through the air, knocking him down with a smack from his serpent tail. Theo landed on the ground with a thud.

"Theo! NO!" Maera screamed, but her father dragged her back toward the shadows. Bradly landed with a louder thud, still in his serpent-like dragon body. "Theo!" Maera cried out. "Get up! You can fight him! You fought cancer! You fought pirates, zombies, and a crazy doctor! You can do this, Theo! Just believe in yourself!"

"Maera, leave him be. We're going," the king declared.

"Letting your girlfriend stand up for you?" Bradly laughed. "How pathetic."

"You're just a nightmare!" Theo screamed, getting back to his feet.

"Poor little cancer boy, losing his hair and now his leg," Bradly taunted.

"Shut up!" Theo yelled. "You're nothing but a nightmare! An ugly, mean nightmare!" Theo glared at Bradly, and then suddenly, he reached down and pulled out a sword. In one moment, there was nothing there. Then, in the next, it appeared, strapped to Theo's side like when they were on the pirate ship.

The last thing Maera saw before her father whisked her away into the shadows was Theo fighting back, wielding his sword the way the pirates had taught him. That was when the shadows swallowed her and her father up, transporting them back to the castle. They stood on the balcony with the giant hourglass. There was less red sand inside than ever before. Maera frowned. It reminded her of Theo and the threat her father had made that she wouldn't see him again. Time was running out.

"Take me back! I want to help him!" Maera demanded, "He's my friend, and you just left him there to face that bully alone! You don't know what he's been through! I have to help him! I have to!"

"No," the king said with finality.

"It's not fair," Maera sulked.

"Life often isn't fair, Maera," the king pointed out.

She scowled at him, still feeling angry but wanting answers. "Why can't I go to the Roads of Wreckage?"

"For the very reason that you found yourself stuck inside that car, Maera," her father answered calmly.

His answers only caused her mind to flood with more questions. "And why did the nightmare capture me and place me in the car? I thought nightmares couldn't hurt me since I live here!" Maera exclaimed, wanting to lash out at him for how unfair it all was.

"Not all nightmares follow the rules I set," the king replied. "When you don't follow the rules, that's what happens. I have rules for a reason, and those rules keep you safe. You're not ready to face the Roads of Wreckage. When you are, that nightmare won't bother you anymore. Until then, stay away."

"And what if Theo isn't ready to face Bradly, the bully?" Maera shot back, still worried about her friend.

"Then you won't ever see him again," her father bluntly stated.

"You can't do that!" She was close to crying. "You don't understand! He needs me!"

"I do understand," he replied. "More than you even know. As king, I have watched over Sleepers for eons. Their dreams reveal to me truths of the lives they lead in the Waking World. I have seen hardship, I have seen struggles, and I know what people fear most. Do you think that was the first time I have seen a little boy run from a bully? Do you think I have not seen the nightmares children have? Do you think that I am heartless for not stepping in?"

"Yes," Maera shot back, and the king sighed sadly.

"Preventing children from facing their fears will only ever hold them back. Life is hard, Maera. Their dreams and nightmares help them grow up and learn how to overcome those hardships. They help them figure out who they are and how to make sense of the world. Theo must learn for himself, Maera. You cannot fight his battles for him. After all, you have your own to face, as we all do. It is my duty to ensure that this realm prepares Sleepers for the real challenges they'll face out there in the Waking World. It is not an easy job, but it is my duty, nonetheless. It is because I care that I continue to do it."

"But he's my friend," Maera whispered.

"And he must do this on his own. That is the way this will go, and that's final."

Maera glared at her father, but she could see he wouldn't budge on this. "I won't forgive you for this," Maera declared, then ran out of the room.

Once she was in her own room, she slammed the door shut and threw herself on her bed as she cried. She cried because she wasn't sure if Theo could face his nightmare. She cried because she was scared that it was the last time she'd ever see him. She cried because she had no purpose in Nightmare and was different from all the other Wonders. When the tears slowed, she cried anew, growing certain that the only way she'd find her purpose was if she went back to the awful street in the Roads of Wreckage where the accident happened, and she wasn't sure she could face that again... not without her friend.

Eventually, the tears ran out, and in her despair and sadness, Maera fell asleep, staying asleep for a long time. Many days and nights passed, and yet Maera didn't wake up.

When Maera finally opened her eyes, she felt like she'd been sleeping for ages, but something had changed. Something pulled her from her deep sleep. She glanced around the room and noticed it was different. This one was strangely bright. It looked like her room in the castle but also the opposite. Instead of dark purple walls, these walls were a soft, bright purple... like lilacs. Instead of her dark blue bedding, the bedding was sky-blue and cheery with white sheets and pillows. Sunshine streamed in through the window instead of red skies and dark clouds.

Where am I? Why aren't I in Nightmare?

"What the...!" She got out of bed and opened the door. The hallways weren't black like the halls in the obsidian castle of Nightmare; they were white. She looked at the door, and it did have 311 carved into it with fancy lettering.

"Good! You're awake!" A beautiful princess clapped her delicate hands together from where she sat in the corner, flashing a perfect, bright smile with overly white teeth. If this was her room back in Nightmare, it would have been Alessandra checking on her. Instead, this girl looked like a Barbie doll—something Maera despised. The princess wore a hideous, soft pink, sparkling ballroom gown—the top of which had a darker pink lace over the glittery material. She had glossy brown hair, done up with braids, curls, and fancy hairpins, complete with pearls and rhinestones. It made Maera nauseous to look at her.

"The queen has requested that I take you to her," the princess said in a sing-song voice, grating on Maera's ears.

"The queen?" Maera blinked, feeling utterly confused.

"Yes, the Queen of Dreams. This way, please," the princess said in her annoyingly pleasant voice. She turned and gracefully led the way out of the room.

Maera stalked after her, finding the princess irritating with how gracefully and perfectly she walked in that massive, poofy pink gown. She even smelled like roses, the sweet kind, not like the repugnant ones in Nightmare.

When they reached the throne room, the princess stopped, urging Maera to continue.

"Maera! You're finally up. I'm so glad." The queen smiled radiantly from her throne. "Someone has been asking about you."

Maera stood before the queen and gave a small curtsey. "How did I get here?" Maera asked when she straightened. "Who's asking about me here in Dream?"

The queen laughed, a beautiful sound, almost like tinkling bells. "Maera, you're here because I summoned you, of course. You've been asleep for a long while, and I thought it was time you woke up."

"But the king...," Maera began.

The queen smiled. "Dear sweet girl, the king is only one part of the Land of Dreams, and his kingdom is only one-half. Do *I* not get a say in what happens here? After all, I am *also* part of this place. He governs a part of this realm, watching over Nightmare, just as I help govern what happens here in Dream. Together, we watch over the entirety of the Land of Dreams and all who are in it. Things around here have been changing, Maera, but in some ways, they are not changing enough. So, doesn't it make sense that I should also have some say over what's happening?"

"I... suppose you do get a say," Maera replied, not entirely sure she understood what all the queen meant.

The queen smiled kindly as if she understood. "What many don't realize is that the kingdoms of Dream and Nightmare work *together*, my dear. Our common goal is to ensure that *everyone* and *everything* inside the Land of Dreams gets the most out of being here. That means King Nightmare knows that you're here, young Maera, and has allowed this meeting to take place. Now come, follow me. Someone has been waiting a long time to see you."

The queen rose from the throne in one graceful motion, and then she glided down the stairs of the platform. "This way, my dear girl," the queen said in her sing-song voice.

Maera followed her, exiting the throne room through a side door. They continued until they reached a dazzling courtyard with the most vibrant and brightest roses Maera had ever seen. There were brilliant yellow ones with pink-tipped petals, white and hot pink ones, and a few soft purple roses as well. All left the air perfumed and smelling sweet. Glowing rainbow butterflies fluttered about; the edges of their wings displayed a shimmering white that separated the various colors of blues, pinks, greens, yellows, and purples. Maera watched the colorful creatures as they fluttered from one flower to the next.

"Why am I here? And who's asking for me?" Maera asked, feeling impatient and out of place.

"Yes, follow me, and you'll soon see. I think it will be such a wonderful surprise for you." The queen led Maera toward a fountain in the center of the courtyard. Then her eyes fell on someone sitting down at the fountain, and Maera could hardly believe it.

"Theo!" Maera ran to her friend.

Once he saw her, he stood and hurried toward her as best as

he could with his prosthetic leg before they collided in a hug. "Maera! It's really you!"

"I thought the nightmare would have kept you away from me!" she cried. "I thought that I wasn't going to see you again. My father said that unless you beat the nightmare, I would never see you."

"But I *did* beat it," Theo replied with twinkling blue eyes. "I stood up to Bradly. When I used the sword, the moment I beat him, he disappeared in a poof of glowing red sand. I haven't had a nightmare since, and it's been *months*, Maera."

"Months?" Maera questioned. "It has?"

"Yes. I kept forgetting my dreams! The thing is, whenever I met the queen here in Dream, she said we often forget our dreams, so I had the hardest time figuring out how to get to you. With you being in Nightmare, I haven't been able to cross over, and I did try. For some reason, since facing my nightmare, I haven't been able to get past the mountains bordering Nightmare, and since I was stuck in Dream, I kept forgetting. Finally, I had to ask for the queen's help!"

"That's crazy," Marea said as she pulled away. "I... didn't realize." She looked at the queen, who smiled.

"He may have forgotten his dreams," the queen chimed in, her smile growing, "but each time he came here, he's asked about you."

"Right," Theo nodded. "At first, no one could reach you. Then she discovered you'd fallen into some strange sleep you couldn't wake from. The king was glad that she was willing to help to wake you. It took the joint effort of both her *and* the king to get you here."

"Really?" Maera looked at the queen.

The queen nodded. "The king said you refused to awaken, so, with his assistance, we finally brought you here to Dream to see if a change in setting would help. It's fortunate you finally awoke. You had us all worried. Time is such a funny thing... there never seems to be enough of it," she mused mysteriously. "No matter, you've come out of it, and that's the important thing. Now, I'm sure that you both have a lot to talk about, so I'll leave you to it." The elegant woman glided away, leaving the two children to talk in the garden.

"I'm so sorry it took me this long to see you again," Theo said once they were alone.

"It's okay," Maera replied quietly, feeling a little troubled. "I'm just so glad you beat the nightmare; I was so worried."

"I thought I'd never see you again," Theo confessed. "Maera, there's something I need to tell you. I'm finally cancer-free! They got it all!"

"That's wonderful, Theo!" Maera smiled, her heart lifting.

"And another thing," Theo said, his face growing serious. "The ghost girl in room 311... they're going to pull the plugs in a matter of days. I came to warn you."

Maera's brows knitted together in perplexion. "Why are you telling me this?"

"I'm telling you because that girl *is* you. The last time I visited, the old man was talking to her, holding her hand. He called the girl *Maera*."

"He?"

"The old man who visits room 311... he is your grandpa, Maera, and *you're* the *ghost girl*. My friends at the hospital said they'd seen you in their dreams sometimes... well, in their nightmares. You'd appear in the halls of the hospital, the same one where they took my foot. They remembered you from *their* nightmares of the hospital. You always watched, standing at the edges like a ghost, and then you disappeared. I guess that's when you went to live at the castle in Nightmare."

"How... how is that possible?" Maera could scarcely believe it.

"I can only remember my life in Nightmare. I've been there for many, many years."

"You're asleep because you were in an accident—a car accident. A truck had run a stop sign and hit the car you were in. Your parents died, but you didn't. You're in a coma, and you have been for three years. I guess time doesn't work the same in your dreams as it does in the real world."

"No, it doesn't," Maera shook her head. "But there's no way I'm her! I can't be. I was *born* in Nightmare."

"Are you sure you were actually *born* there?" Theo asked. "What if you were just a Sleeper who'd been there for a really long time? You might not remember because of the accident."

"No. That... that's impossible. My father—he would have told me," Maera insisted.

"Would he? Could he? The queen said that their role is to help each of us find our path and discover things for ourselves. What if he couldn't tell you?"

"No, something that big, he would've," Maera argued. "And I live in Nightmare. I belong there, Theo. That's where I was born. It's the only thing that makes sense."

"Is it? Maybe the accident prevented you from remembering. Maybe you've been stuck there for so long that you forgot who you are. You're a Sleeper, Maera, just like me." His words pierced her chest like shards of ice, making it hard to breathe.

"No," Maera backed away. "You're lying."

"I wouldn't lie to you," he frowned.

"What you're saying doesn't make any sense, though!"

Except Theo wasn't deterred by this. "Let me ask you this, then. Did the king ever actually say you *were* born there?"

Maera thought about it. She thought back on all the conversations she and her father had ever had and realized the king had never once admitted to creating her. He'd never really said aloud that she'd been born from the sand like other Wonders, just that she lived in Nightmare like them.

"I... I don't know," Maera whispered. "But what about my purpose? He said to find my purpose like other Wonders do."

"Except they always have a job to do from the moment that they're born, but you never did. You're different from them, Maera. Why is that?"

"I don't know," Maera frowned. "I just don't know!" She didn't like talking about this.

"Maybe that purpose is to wake up," Theo told her. "Maybe your purpose is to remember. Maybe your purpose is to *live*."

"Stop," Maera backed away. "I don't want to hear anymore. I'm a Wonder, and I belong in Nightmare."

"No, you don't, Maera, you need to wake up. You're running out of time!" Theo argued impatiently.

It made her think about something her father had said at the Roads of Wreckage. *"Time is running out, and certain lessons have yet to be learned...."*

"You have to wake up, Maera. You have to!" Theo pleaded with desperation.

"Stop! I won't hear anymore!" Tears filled her eyes, and Maera turned and ran.

"Maera! You need to wake up! That's what I've come to tell you!" Theo hollered after her. "Maera!"

Maera didn't stop. She sprouted her silver wings and lifted off into the air.

"I'll prove it," she told herself. "I just need to go to the Roads of Wreckage. Once I face it, I'll learn what my purpose is, and I'll know the truth!"

"Maera!" Theo's voice grew distant, but she didn't stop. She couldn't. She had to learn the truth, one way or another.

Maera flew over Dream and then soared over the Frosting Mountains. Once she crossed into Nightmare, she passed over the Mountains of Terror. She flew over the Haunted Plain, and soon she swooped down, flying low until she reached the Roads of Wreckage. When she landed on the wet road in the rain, she marched up to the crossroads. The moment she stepped onto the pavement, the nightmare reappeared. She watched it play out the same way it had before. The truck ran the stop sign, hitting the car, causing it to flip over and over, landing upside down in the rain. This particular nightmare replayed over and over.

Maera straightened her shoulders, determined to face this head-on. Mustering her courage, she walked up to the front of the car this time. When she looked at the people inside, she was transported to the back seat... the car was moving, and the crash hadn't happened yet.

"Maera, turn that down," a familiar voice said. Maera held a tablet while she watched a cartoon; it was playing a little too loudly. She recognized the movie but couldn't quite remember the name. The noise of the movie drowned out the tapping of the rain on the car. The *swish, swish* of the windshield wipers was part of the symphony of white noise that her cartoon attempted to drown out. Maera ignored the order to turn it down and continued watching her movie.

"Maera, turn it down, I said." The woman in the front seat turned around, and Maera looked up at her face. She knew this woman.

"What, Mom?"

She blinked. *This all feels so familiar....*

"Turn it down, sweetie. It's too loud," her mom urged.

"Listen to your mother," the man who was driving said.

Dad? Maera knew these people. Somehow, she had forgotten, but suddenly she knew that these were her parents. She looked around; she knew this car too. They pulled up to the stop sign. It was raining and dark. The sound of her movie filled the car with noise. She fiddled with the volume button.

"Mare Bear, it's still too loud," her dad said as he pulled forward, glancing at her through the rear-view mirror.

Before Maera could turn it down more, bright light filled the interior of the car. If light could be sound, then this light was louder than all the other noises, including her show. For a moment, the light was all she could think about. It was *blinding*.

In the next breath, the truck collided with the car.

Her parents hadn't seen it coming; they were too focused on her.

This was my fault.

It all happened so fast.

The sound of the crash was a tragic melody of the loudest and most startling sounds that Maera had ever heard. The sound of metal twisting and glass tinkling ended with a deafening thud that caused the car to flip over and over. The sudden and abrupt attack seemed to last too long, almost as if time slowed down before it sped up again.

When the car finally stopped moving, it landed upside down, and Maera felt a trickle of blood drip up her face. Her parents didn't move, and the smell of something burning filled Maera's nose.

"Mommy?" Maera called out in a panicked voice. "Dad? Daddy? Help! Daddy, I'm stuck." Maera struggled in her seat, but her seat belt was stuck, and she remembered... *everything*.

Tears filled her eyes, running up her head. She hung helplessly from the seat in their upside-down mangled car. It was dark, and the smell of smoke wafted through the broken windows.

The *tap, tap, tap* of rain was louder than the distant sound of her cartoon that continued playing from somewhere outside of the car.

Maera remembered being afraid–terrified.

Why aren't my mommy and daddy talking to me? Why aren't they moving?

"Someone...," she cried. "Help me. It hurts really bad." She didn't know where she was hurt, only that it did, and that made her even more afraid as she hung suspended upside down while her parents stayed silent. "Mommy? Daddy?" she sobbed, "I'm stuck. Please help. Please."

She remembered.

Maera didn't want to be there.

"I'm scared...." She remembered wanting to forget. She wanted to get away from this terrible nightmare. Her head and her body hurt so bad... until she fell asleep.

CHAPTER

THIRTEEN

"I found you like this," the King of Nightmares said. He knelt outside the rear window of the car. "You were crying and afraid. Strangely, you didn't remember who you were or where you came from. I tried waking you up to send you back to the Waking World, but my power wouldn't work on you."

"They're dead," Maera said as tears fell from her eyes. She stood beside the car, next to the man she had called her father. She remembered her real parents now, and she also knew they were gone.

The King of Nightmare placed a gentle hand on her shoulder. "They are, and when you didn't wake up, I decided to keep an eye on you. At first, you visited the Crumbling Hospital. You spent a lot of time in the children's ward and tried talking to the kids who appeared there in their nightmares. I thought perhaps they might help you wake up. When that didn't happen, I took you in and showed you all of Nightmare. You were the first Sleeper in ages who actually *liked* being here in Nightmare. So, I brought you home to live in the castle. I wanted to show you everything, and I wanted to protect you... I knew you'd fit right in. I've cared for you as if you were my daughter, and I've loved you like a daughter. You're a special girl, Maera. My little Night Maera."

"Why didn't you tell me who I was?" she sniffed.

"I couldn't. That was for you to discover." He held her hand and pulled her into the shadows. They reappeared on the balcony with the large hourglass. "I thought you had enough time to figure it out," the king explained. "However, the sand is running out. When you are near the hourglass, it only shows the sand *you* create, but I see *all* the sand from *all* the Sleepers who come to Nightmare. All this sand you see in there now is from you, Maera. The things you've created in your mind, the Sands of Imagination, are all your ideas ever since you've been here. Unfortunately, the sand is not as plentiful as it once was, and with the passing of time, there is less and less. When that boy, Theo, arrived, I knew he might be the one who would change things. When you both were together, more sand was made."

"What do you mean, he might be the one?" Maera asked.

"I thought that perhaps he would be the one who could help you face what you needed to face," the king answered. "That he would help you learn the truth and that you'd finally be able to wake up."

"Then why forbid me to see him?" Maera asked in confusion.

The king laughed, but his eyes remained sad. "Well, because anytime I forbade you from doing something, you always did it anyway. I had hoped my restrictions would help push you to discover things on your own. And it worked."

"I remember now," Maera confessed, and her heart hurt knowing the terrible truth. "I remember everything."

"Yes, I knew this day would come," the king said sadly. "The day you would leave here."

"And my mom and dad are gone," she whispered.

"Yes. For that, I'm very sorry," the king said softly.

"What's going to happen to me now?" Maera asked, looking up into those wise, silver eyes of his.

"You need to wake up, my sweet girl. You don't have much time left." He pointed to the hourglass. There were very few grains of sand inside.

"But... what about you? I don't want to leave you; you have been my father. I don't want to leave Nightmare, Colossal, or Hagetha, or any of my other Wonders."

Maera knew he wasn't her real dad, but she'd come to love him like a father. Her real father and mother were now dead... Maera didn't want to lose him too.

"Ah, my dear, little Night Maera. You must understand that the more often you return, the longer we'll all stay. I will *always* be here for you for as long as you need me to be."

Maera wrapped her arms around the King of Nightmare, burying her face in his cloak of shadows and stars. "I don't want to leave you," she cried.

The king wrapped his long arms around his little Night Maera and whispered, "But you must, Maera." He gently brushed back her hair. "You've finally learned everything you needed from me. You've finally faced your fears and remembered who you are. You let your nightmare teach you how to face those fears. You're ready now, and it's time for you to finally wake up."

"I don't want to. Can't I stay here? Don't you want me?"

"Oh, my sweet girl," he said with sorrowful eyes. "You will always be my little Night Maera, and though I wish you could stay here forever, I know that you need to wake up. You see, I don't want you to disappear forever, and if you remain here and don't wake up, you really could disappear. Time is running out, so you must be brave for me one more time and wake up. I know this is hard, but I also know you can do this."

"What if I forget? The queen said we sometimes forget our dreams!" Maera didn't want to go, nor did she want to forget.

"It's going to be okay," he soothed. "I love you, and I will always be here for you whenever you need me. All you have to do is dream."

"But I'm scared," Maera murmured tearfully.

"You can do this," the king said. "You're brave. Just think about all the exciting adventures you're going to have in the Waking World, a place not even Wonders can go. I want you to have those adventures. A parent always wants the best for their children, and though you might be sad for a while, eventually, that sadness will fade, and you'll be happy." She hugged him tighter, not wanting to let him go. Eventually, he pulled away and then wiped away her tears.

"It's time," he said as he glanced at the hourglass. He tapped his staff to the glass at the base, and the last bits of her sand floated upward, flashing and turning into red light, which quickly absorbed into the red orb of his staff. Then he began waving it in the air, and the red light surrounded her like wisps of bright, glowing smoke.

"I love you, Maera. Be brave. Be strong. Now, wake up." He tapped her with the staff, and a brilliant burst of red light exploded, and then everything disappeared.

Maera woke up to the sound of a steady *beep, beep, beep*. She was in a hospital; it wasn't the Crumbling Hospital. It was clean and quiet. She felt as if she had woken from the most wonderful dream... but it began to fade, as dreams often do. She didn't quite remember why she was in a hospital. She turned her head and saw her grandfather sitting quietly next to her bed; his head was bowed as he prayed for her to wake up.

"Pap Pap?" she croaked. Her throat was sore; it was as if she hadn't used her voice in a very long time.

His head snapped up, and he looked at her in with wide eyes. "Maer Bear?" His eyes filled with tears. "You're awake!" He gently stroked her cheek.

"Where's Mommy and Daddy?" she asked, looking around.

His face fell.

Just then, a ghost of a memory told her that she wouldn't see them again, but she couldn't recall why.

"You were in a terrible accident. They... didn't make it–they went to Heaven," he said softly. "I'm so sorry. You... you've been asleep for a long time, Maera. I didn't know if you were ever going to wake up. Oh, sweetheart, I'm so glad that you did! I'm going to call the nurse!" Her grandpa raced to the door and yelled into the hall. "I need a nurse! Or a doctor!"

Suddenly, some nurses hurried in. Everyone raced around Maera, fussing over her and looking at the numbers on the beeping monitor while checking her vitals. They said they needed to get the doctor and left nearly as quickly as they had come.

Eventually, the doctor came.

Maera stared in surprise. "Doc?" He looked very familiar, and she half expected his smile to split open his face.

"I can't believe it. This is a miracle," the doctor said with a boringly normal mouth. "The scans didn't indicate that you would wake up. How do you feel? Do you know where you are?"

"I'm...," she frowned, glancing around, "at the hospital?"

"Yes," he smiled blandly while he checked her wrist and looked at his watch. "And do you remember your name?"

"Maera," she replied.

"Very good," he said, with bright eyes. "You've beaten the odds. Amazing. In all my years...." he shook his head and then finished looking her over.

"Is she going to be okay now that she's awake? When can she go home?" her grandpa asked.

"We'll keep her a little longer for observations. I also want to run some scans and see how her condition has changed since the accident."

Maera tuned out the grown-up talk. It was too confusing, and she didn't understand any of it. She felt a set of eyes on her, and she glanced at the open door to her room.

A blond-haired boy with blue eyes and an artificial leg smiled at her from the doorway. "Maera?" the boy murmured hesitantly.

She remembered. She knew this boy! "Theo?" Maera sat up, and Theo came limping into the room. "Theo!"

Theo smiled the biggest smile she had seen, and his eyes lit with relieved joy. "You're awake! You did it!"

"What is he talking about?" her grandfather asked as he gazed at the two children exchanging their greetings.

"Theo, he's my friend. He found me in the Land of Dreams. He helped me wake up," Maera explained.

The doctor frowned. "There may be some lasting damage," the doctor remarked. "But we can do an MRI and a CAT scan to make sure everything's okay."

"You don't believe her," Theo stated, "but she's telling the truth, Doc."

"It's just... it sounds a bit unbelievable, kiddo, even though she *is* awake now," the doctor said reluctantly.

"I'd like to hear all about it," her grandfather said. "This boy never gave up on her, and he visited her when no one else did."

"I'll go ahead and give you some privacy while I order those tests," the doctor commented before leaving the room.

Maera and Theo told her grandfather all about their adventures in the Land of Dreams. The tales included zombies, witches, pirates, cotton candy clouds, and mad dragons. Her grandpa believed her.

"You know…," her grandfather said thoughtfully, "I sometimes visited a cave in my dreams. I walked through it, and it led to this sort of haunted oasis in the mountains. There was blue-green grass and black, skeletal unicorns. I also remember a few flying black horses, and there was this strange, green waterfall that emptied into a putrid green river that cut through this grassy meadow."

"We've been there!" Theo chirped.

"I believe you," her grandpa said. "What's stranger still, it wasn't really a nightmare. Not to me, at least. It was the *only* place I'd see Maera. She wasn't always there, but sometimes she was."

"I remember you!" She suddenly smiled. "But I didn't know it was you, Pap Pap."

"I'm so glad you're awake, Maer Bear." Her grandpa hugged her and kissed her head. "You're going to come live with me now."

Maera left the hospital a couple of days later and lived with her grandfather in Point Defiance, which wasn't far from where Theo lived. They became the best of friends and even attended the same school.

Theo stood up to Bradly, the bully, and Maera stood by his side, ready to defend her friend. That year was one of the best years Maera had.

Maera missed her parents, but she sometimes saw them in her dreams. She also dreamed of a tall man who wore a shadowy cloak covered in nebulas and stars. He often held a wooden staff with a red orb. True to his word, the King of Nightmares was there for her as long as she needed him. Each time she dreamed of him, she talked about all the things she'd done since waking up.

However, like most dreams, the best ones faded with time. Little by little, she grew up, and her time in Nightmare became a distant memory. Each new year and every new experience birthed new dreams, and the dreams Maera created were some of the best and wildest of them all.

Maera's dreams were inspired by the games she and Theo played in the Waking World, and they played many games. Sometimes, they pretended to ride on the backs of giant butterflies. Other times, they sailed on a ship made from cardboard boxes and pretended to be part of a crew of pirates. Once, they fought dragons and serpents using sticks for swords.

Maera had many adventures, and though some dreams faded, she kept many close to her heart. Somehow, she was never scared when she had a nightmare. Instead, she felt like she was going home, returning to a realm where she was the Princess of Nightmare, a place where Wonders were born and helped people overcome their challenges and face their fears. Because of Nightmare, she had many friends who were a dream away; she had found love in loss, and she learned how to be brave when afraid. Most of all, she found a best friend who'd helped her as much as she helped him. She learned to never underestimate the power of love and friendship. Sometimes, that was all that was needed to work up the courage to face the impossible.

Through her experiences in Nightmare, Maera discovered her true purpose, which was to empower others by showing them how to face their fears and find their strengths. She bravely lived her life to the fullest and never once stopped dreaming.

The End

Acknowledgments

A big thanks to my husband, Michael, for being my rock through every obstacle and challenge I faced on this journey. You are the love of my life, and your unwavering support has meant the world to me. I would not have made it this far without you.

Another big thanks to my mom, who has spent countless hours helping me edit and refine this story until it was a more presentable manuscript. I still cannot believe you aren't tired of me calling on you for help yet! Thanks for being the one I can run to whenever I am stuck, even if it's just to bounce ideas off you. You have been there from the very start, and your belief in me that I could actually make it this far means more than you know.

Another big thanks to those who were the first ones to read this, being my test audience, and helping to locate any missed errors or making suggestions that moved the story along.

I also wanted to personally thank my amazing editor, Stacey, who has been my friend and coach, answering countless questions and helping to get this story off the ground and out into the world. Lastly, I wanted to thank my readers who made the success of this story possible.

ABOUT THE AUTHOR

Alecia is a writer, an artist, and an overthinker.

Since winning a class competition for best story in first grade, she has discovered a love for stories. As a child, there was nothing more exciting than ordering a new book from the school catalogs, and now, she probably has more books than shelf space.

Throughout her life, Alecia has moved around from place to place until finally settling in Idaho where she is happily married and the proud mamma of four fur babies.

Much of her inspiration comes from dreams, though sometimes her stories stem from a wish to read a book not yet written.

When she isn't cozied up with a good book, she enjoys the outdoors, rock-hounding and foraging, as well as occasionally indulging in playing music or creating art.

You can find her at:
www.AleciaGodin.com

* 9 7 9 8 9 9 1 3 9 6 7 2 1 *